1

THE ADVENTURES

TRAVELS
IN
AFRICA

OF THE

KERRIGAN KIDS

PAINTED WARRIORS & WILD LIONS

THE ADVENTURES OF THE KERRIGAN KIDS

TRAVELS IN AFRICA

PAINTED WARRIORS & WILD LIONS

GILBERT MORRIS

MOODY PRESS
CHICAGO

© 2001 by
GILBERT MORRIS

Library of Congress Cataloging-in-Publication Data

Morris, Gilbert
  Painted warriors and wild lions : travel in Africa / Gilbert Morris.
    p. cm. -- (Adventures of the Kerrigan kids ; #1)
  Sequel: Buckingham Palace and the crown jewels: travel in England.
  Summary: When Duffy Kerrigan and her adopted brothers and sisters, who all come from different countries, accompany their widowed father on a trip to write about and photograph the Masai people in Africa, she learns that she can accept people without having to approve of what they do.
  ISBN 0-8024-1578-4
  [1. Brothers and sisters--Fiction. 2. Aoption--Fiction. 3. Interracial adoption--Fiction. 4. Single-parent families--Fiction. 5. Masai (African people)--Fiction. 6. Africa--Fiction. 7. Christian life--Fiction.] I. Title.

PZ7.M8279 Pai 2001
[Fic]--dc21

                                                    00-046923

1 3 5 7 9 10 8 6 4 2

Printed in the United States of America

CONTENTS

TROUBLE AT THE KERRIGANS'

Duffy Anne Kerrigan moved down the super-market aisle, shoving the shopping cart before her. She was a leggy girl of eleven and had bright red hair and bright green eyes. She picked up a box of cake mix, and her forehead wrinkled as she began to read the instructions out loud.

She jumped when a voice behind her said, "Can I help you, young lady?"

Turning around quickly, Duffy saw a short, overweight, pleasant-looking young man with a head of bushy black hair. She said, "No, thank you. I'm doing all right. I can do it myself."

He said, "My name's Thad. If you need any help, I stand ready." He seemed to be a clerk, and he gave her a brilliant smile. "This is my first day on the job, and I want to make a good impression on the boss."

Duffy nodded. "OK." She put the mix in the cart and would have walked on, but the black-haired clerk persisted. "Does your mother know you're buying all this stuff?"

After a moment's silence, Duffy said through tight lips, "My mother died three months ago."

The young man blinked and bit his lip. "Well, I'm sorry for saying anything, then," he apologized. "But if you do need any help, just—"

At that moment a great crash drowned out his words.

They both whirled around to see that a boy—apparently one who had been pushing a shopping cart at full speed—had encountered a stack of canned green beans. The cans now lay scattered all over the supermarket floor.

"Hey, you, kid!" the clerk yelled and headed toward the boy. "You can't play with those carts. That's not what they're for!"

The boy—he was about ten—had black hair and dark eyes and was sturdily built. He stared up innocently at the clerk and said, "I'm sorry. I didn't mean to do it. I'll put 'em back up."

"You just leave those cans alone! You'll only make the mess worse. Now take what you came for and get out of this store."

Duffy went to them quickly. "He didn't mean to do it. I'll help him put them back," she offered.

"You stay out of this. He's no concern of yours."

"But . . . well . . . yes, he is," Duffy said. "That's Juan. And he's my brother."

The clerk stared at the dark-skinned boy. Then he stared at redheaded Duffy Anne Kerrigan. He said, "He can't be."

At that moment a little girl trotted up the supermarket aisle and joined them. She was oriental looking and had small, beautiful features. Her hair was coal black, and her eyes were almond shaped. "What's the matter?" she asked rather timidly.

The clerk was still rather put out. He said, "And I suppose this is your aunt."

"No, sir," Duffy said quietly. "This is my sister."

The clerk's face grew red. "I know when somebody's making fun of me, and I won't put up with it."

At that moment a tall black boy, wearing a pair of green shorts and a white T-shirt, joined them from the other direction. His eyes were a rich dark brown, and his hair formed a kinky mat on his head. "And what may I ask is going on?" There was a British sound to his voice.

"Is all this any of your business?" the clerk Thad demanded.

"Yes, it really is," Duffy said. "He's my brother, too."

The clerk glared at the four of them and then muttered, "Kids got no respect for their elders these days."

Since Thad could not have been more than eighteen himself, he was not very elder, but he was obviously still angry. "All you kids get what you need and leave, and don't give me any more of that brother-sister stuff, either!"

Whirling about, Thad walked down the aisle muttering to himself.

At the checkout counter, the grocery clerk Thad went to the checker, a tall woman with gray hair. "Amanda," he grumped, "kids just got no respect for their elders these days."

"What are you talking about?" the older woman asked. She had no customers at the moment, and she seemed prepared to listen to his complaints.

"You see those kids over there? There. By the vegetable counter."

"Sure. Those are the Kerrigan kids."

At that moment, the manager, Mr. Stoval, came by and heard what she said. "They're a nice family, the Kerrigans," he said.

Thad felt befuddled. "But they're all different colors," he said. "They're different nationalities."

"That's right," Mr. Stoval said. "They are. I've known Mr. Kerrigan for a long time—his wife too while she was alive. Jim Kerrigan and I grew up together. He's famous in a way."

"Famous for what?" Thad asked.

"Well, he writes stories, and then he takes pictures of all kinds of faraway places. And the stuff gets published."

"You mean he writes books?"

"So far," Mr. Stoval said, "he sells stories to magazines—like the *National Geographic* and periodicals like that."

"The redhead said her mother died."

Sadness came into Mr. Stoval's eyes. "That's right," he said. "Mrs. Kerrigan died just three months ago. Fine, fine lady. Really sad. Everyone at the church misses her."

"But these kids—how come—"

"Well, the Kerrigans wanted a house full of children. But Duffy was an only child. So a few years ago, they started adopting children."

"But they're not—well, they're not *American*."

"They're not. They came from orphanages all over the world. That one there is from Mexico. He's ten. And that black boy beside him is from Nigeria. His name is Seth. The little girl is from Hong Kong. I don't know her name in Chinese, but it means Pearl in English, so that's what they call her."

Thad suddenly felt greatly ashamed of himself. "Well, I didn't know. I gave them kind of a hard time."

"Well, you don't want to do that again," Mr. Stoval said. "They're having a hard enough time after losing their mother." He frowned and added, "Jim Kerrigan is having an awful time trying to be

11

a father and a mother at the same time. Now, that is really rough!"

In the Kerrigan kitchen, Duffy narrowed her eyes as she studied the instructions on the cake mix box. Then she took two round cake pans from the cupboard and greased and floured them. She opened the box of mix and poured the contents into a bowl. She measured the water and the oil, poured them into the bowl, and then cracked in one egg.

About the time she had the cake batter ready for the mixer, Juan came in. "What's happening, Duffy?"

"What does it look like?"

"It looks like you're making a cake."

"Well, aren't you smart, Juan?" Duffy said absently. "Now, don't you get in my way."

"I think I'll learn to cook myself," Juan said. He grinned and punched Duffy on the arm.

"Stop hitting on me," she complained. "You don't know how hard you hit."

"Oh, I'm sorry," Juan said. His white teeth flashed against his olive skin. "I won't do it again until the next time." His eyes suddenly sparkled, and he said, "Hey, Duffy. Do you know what the name of the prophet's horse was?"

"No, I don't. What prophet? And I didn't even know the prophet had a horse." Juan loved jokes. In Duffy's opinion, most of them were terrible.

But she sighed and said, "All right. What was the name of the prophet's horse?"

"His name was Is Me."

"*Is Me!* That doesn't make any sense."

"Sure it does." Juan began to laugh. "The prophet said, 'Whoa, Is Me.'"

It was no worse than most of Juan's terrible jokes, and Duffy merely said, "All right. Now, you just stay out of the way." She left the bowl of batter sitting on the mixer and walked to the refrigerator.

Juan said, "I'll help with this!"

"No, don't do that!" Duffy yelled. But it was too late.

Juan lowered the beaters into the bowl and switched on the mixer, which, unfortunately, was set on the highest speed. Instantly the cake batter seemed to explode.

"Hey!" Juan yelled. "I can't see!" Cake batter was running down his face. It was all over the front of his clothing. It was on the walls, the ceiling, and it was in Duffy's hair.

"Now see what you've done! You've ruined everything!" Duffy screamed. She always did have too warm a temper, her father said. She flew at Juan.

But Juan was blinded by the cake batter. He couldn't see her coming. Then he slipped on some that had splashed on the floor. He went down with Duffy on top of him.

13

"You've ruined *everything!*" she cried again, beating on him with her fist.

"Stop hitting me! I can't see!"

How much damage Duffy might have done to Juan was impossible to say, for at that moment their father entered the kitchen. Mr. Kerrigan stared at his two children rolling on the floor. He probably also noted the chocolate cake batter on the walls and the ceiling.

"What's going on here?" Mr. Kerrigan asked. He leaned over them, took a firm hold on Duffy, and pulled her off her brother. "Just what are you doing, Duffy?"

"Look what he did, Dad," Duffy said almost in tears. "Look what he did. I was making a cake, and he stuck the beaters into it on high speed."

Juan got to his feet and began wiping the batter out of his eyes. He was a sorry sight. "It wasn't my fault," he said. "It was her fault. She shouldn't have had the mixer set on high speed."

The two began shouting. Suddenly Duffy burst into tears and ran out of the room.

"Juan, that was not a very smart thing to do," Mr. Kerrigan said when Duffy was gone. He ran both hands through his tousled brown hair. He had hair that would never stay combed. "You'd better make things right with Duffy."

"Aw, Dad," Juan said. "I'm the one that got the

batter in the face. She didn't get hardly anything on her."

"I know, but Duffy is upset anyway. She has a lot on her mind these days."

Juan had the batter wiped away from his eyes by now. He looked up into his father's face. "Me too, Dad," he said quietly. "What's going to happen to all of us?"

"I don't know, Juan, but we can't go on as we have been. Not with the kind of work I do . . ."

Juan knew that his dad's work took him to faraway places, and he was often gone for weeks at a time. That had been no problem while their mother was there to take care of the house and the children. But now that she was gone, it was a big problem indeed.

What would happen when school started in September and Dad had to leave on one of his business trips?

Juan saw that his father was worried. He said quickly, "I'll apologize to Duffy, Dad. It was a dumb thing to do, and I'll clean up the mess too. I'll do that first."

"That's good, son. You do that. I'll go talk to Duffy myself, while you get at the cleanup."

Duffy was stretched out across her bed crying, while Pearl sat beside her. Pearl was stroking Duffy's hair and making comforting noises.

Duffy heard their father come in. He sat on

her bed too. Then he pulled Duffy up beside him and said, "Now, honey, don't cry. It was just a little thing. Juan's going to tell you he's sorry, and he's cleaning up all the mess right now."

"Everything's going wrong," she sobbed. Then she drew back and said, "Have you got a handkerchief?"

"Sure." Her dad fished in his pocket and drew out one. He wiped her tears himself, then gave the handkerchief to her.

"I'm sorry I blew up, Daddy," she said, sniffing. "It's that awful temper of mine."

"I'm afraid that we all lose it at times," Mr. Kerrigan said. Then he put his other arm around Pearl. "You all right, Pearl?"

"Yes, Daddy," Pearl said. She lifted her eyes to his. "I'm worried, though. What will happen to us when you have to go away? Daddy, what are we going to do?" Then she said, "I miss Mommy."

"So do I, honey. So do I."

"Why did God take her?"

"We don't know, Pearl. We may not know the reason your mother went to be with Jesus until we get to heaven. But we do know that our Father in heaven loves us. And what God does is always right. Always. Even when we can't understand —because God is always wise and good."

For some time the three just sat there with Mr. Kerrigan's arms around both girls.

Then Pearl asked again, "But, Daddy, what *will*

we do? What will happen when you have to go away?"

"God is going to show us. I'm sure of that."

Duffy looked up, sniffling again. "But how long will we have to wait to find out, Dad?"

Their father hugged them both and said, "Until He shows us, Duffy. Until He shows us."

THE BIG
DECISION

All the Kerrigans took turns doing what cooking they knew how to do. Sometimes the food was burned. Sometimes the food wasn't done. Sometimes there wasn't enough. Sometimes there was too much.

Then there was the laundry. The laundry seemed to grow all by itself. Once Juan groaned, "How can so many clothes get so dirty in such a short time?"

"We can be glad it's summer vacation time," Seth answered. He was trying to iron a shirt and not doing very well at it. "When we have to go to school and take care of the house too, I don't think we can handle it." Seth gave his younger brother a glance. "Have you been worried about that, Juan?"

"Well, to tell the truth, I have a little bit." Juan said gloomily, "Something better happen before September."

Seth hung up his shirt and started sorting clothes to put them into the washer. "Pearl keeps saying all the time that God's going to take care of the problem." He held up a shirt that had a fierce-looking green dragon on the front. "This is an awful-looking shirt."

"Yeah, but Duffy likes it. It's her favorite."

"I guess so. No accounting for what people like." He tossed the shirt on the pile and then said with his British accent, "Well, God will make things come out all right, I suppose. As Dad keeps telling us, the Lord is wise and good, and He loves us."

"Hey, you guys, come into the living room for a minute!" their father said from the doorway.

"Sure, Dad," Seth said.

The two boys hurried out of the laundry room. They found Pearl and Duffy already in the living area with their dad.

Juan said, "What's coming down, Dad?"

"Where do you get these expressions, Juan?"

Juan merely grinned. "What's happening, I mean."

Mr. Kerrigan said, "All of you sit down. This is a family meeting."

The Kerrigan kids all sat across from their father, and their eyes were fixed on their dad's face.

He looked very, very serious, Seth thought.

Duffy said, "What's the matter, Dad? Why are we having a family meeting in the middle of the afternoon? Is something wrong?"

"Well, yes and no."

"You mean it's good news, bad news?" Juan asked. "Tell us the good news first."

"All right, I will." Mr. Kerrigan held up a letter and said, "Look at this. It's a letter from the *National Geographic* magazine, asking me to take some pictures and write a story for them." He handed it over to Duffy, who began to read it for herself.

They passed the letter around, and Seth studied it the longest. "That's a lot of money, isn't it, Dad? You can't turn this down."

"I know it's a great deal of money. It would help us a lot. But there's a problem. Look at when they want me to be there."

Seth studied the letter and then looked up at their dad. "The first of next month."

"That's right," Mr. Kerrigan said. "And I just don't see how I can be ready to go that soon."

Duffy plucked the letter from Seth's hand and looked at it again. "Africa," she said. "All the way to Africa. That's a long way."

"It's a long trip all right. I wrote the magazine and told them I wanted to go there and get a photographic history of the Masai people. And as you see, they are interested in using it for the magazine."

"The Masai are the ones who used to be the most fierce warriors in Africa," Seth said. He knew a lot about African history. He said, "Nobody could beat them in the early days before the Europeans came."

"Well, their way of life is vanishing quickly, and I'd like to get it in print and on film before it's gone completely."

For some time the family talked about the offer. Africa seemed a million miles away to most of the Kerrigan kids. Seth, of course, had come from there.

Finally Mr. Kerrigan looked around at the faces of the youngsters and said, "Well, kids, I can't leave you here alone. I'll either have to make some kind of arrangements or turn down the job. But we do need the money, and it's important that I do the story . . ." He hesitated a long moment. Then he said, "What I've decided to do is to get you a baby-sitter."

"A baby-sitter!" Duffy cried. "Who are you going to get to baby-sit us?"

Again there was a hesitation, and finally Mr. Kerrigan said, "Your Aunt Minnie has offered to come and stay with you."

A groan went up instantly from all four children. "Not Aunt Minnie!" they all cried in one form or another. "Not her! Anybody but Aunt Minnie!"

Seth glanced at Duffy and guessed what she

was thinking. *Please, not Aunt Minnie!* Duffy especially could not get along with Aunt Minnie.

"Now, your Aunt Minnie is a good woman. She has a kind heart, and she's made a kind offer," their dad said. "I know she can be rather strict with children but—"

"Dad, it's just that she's just not very good with kids," Duffy cried.

"Duffy's right, Dad," Juan put in. "She's not mean. But she treats us all just like we were grownups. She just doesn't understand kids. She never had any."

"I don't think she was ever a kid herself," Duffy muttered.

"Now that's an unkind thing to say!" Mr. Kerrigan said sharply. "Your aunt means well, and she's made a kind offer, and I can't think of anyone else to help us out." His lips drew into a straight line, and he looked around the circle. "I don't see any other way. Either I stay home, and get a job that won't take me away, and take care of you kids myself—or Aunt Minnie will have to come for a little while."

"Oh me!" Duffy groaned. "I'd just as soon have Attila the Hun."

"Now you stop talking like that about your aunt, young lady," Mr. Kerrigan said firmly.

"All right, Dad. I won't talk it."

But Seth—and probably everyone else—knew what was in Duffy's mind, which was, *But I'll think it.*

"OK. That's it, then. I'll be in touch with Aunt Minnie. How's supper coming along?"

Seth thought their dad looked weary. Dad must have struggled a long time with this big decision.

"It's my turn to fix it tonight. I'm fixing a biblical dish," Juan said, grinning.

But their dad knew Juan very well. "No," he said, "we're not having any jokes about the Bible."

"Anyway, somebody else will have to help Seth finish the ironing if I fix supper," Juan said.

"Pearl and I will fix supper. You do the laundry," Duffy told him.

In the kitchen Pearl said, "Let's make spaghetti. It's easy to make, and everybody likes it."

"All right, let's. You get out lettuce for a salad, Pearl, and I'll fix the spaghetti."

The two girls began working on the meal. After a while Duffy said, "Are you worried, Pearl—about Aunt Minnie coming and all?"

"No."

"You're not? Well, I am."

"You shouldn't be," Pearl said cheerfully. "Jesus said not to worry about anything."

"I don't know how to do that. I can't help being worried. And if she comes, she'll . . . well, you know what Aunt Minnie is like."

Pearl gave Duffy a brilliant smile. "Jesus will fix things," she said in a sure voice. "Jesus can fix anything. All you have to do is ask Him and let Him."

"I suppose you're probably right about that," Duffy admitted. "Sometimes I forget to just trust Him, but I'm getting better at it."

"We've all got to believe in Jesus more." Her sister smiled. "He's the one we can always trust to fix things."

DUFFY'S
MASTER PLAN

Well, it looks like it's Minnie for us," Juan groaned.

He had been strumming on his guitar, and across the room Seth was keeping time with the bass. People said the two of them played very well together. Often they were joined by Duffy. She played both the flute and the piano, and even Pearl was learning to play the drums.

Juan suddenly grinned as though he'd thought of something more pleasant than Aunt Minnie. He said, "Maybe we can be a rock group. We can call ourselves The Awful Truth—"

Seth grinned back at him as his fingers rippled over the strings. "Yeah. Sounds about right to me."

They both chuckled at this, but then Seth's face took on a worried look. "I'm afraid you're right about what's going to happen, though. Looks like it's going to be Aunt Minnie for us."

"I'd just as soon be locked up in Alcatraz."

"Alcatraz is closed," Seth corrected him. "It's a place for tourists to visit now."

"Well, whatever," Juan said gloomily. "But you know what Aunt Minnie's like. I know she means well, but every time she hears us laugh she must say, 'I've got to find out what those kids are doing to have such fun and put a stop to it.'"

"Oh, Aunt Minnie's not that bad! She's all right. It's just that . . ."

Juan and Seth made music together for a while longer, and then their father came in. "That sounds good," he said. "What's the name of it?"

"Doesn't have a name," Juan teased. "We're just making it up as we go along." He looked at his dad's face and thought he was not very happy. "Sit down, Dad. We'll dedicate a song to you. How about 'On Top of Old Smokey'?"

Mr. Kerrigan sank into a chair across from them. "How do you know old songs like that?" he asked.

"They sing them all the time on the country-western station."

"I don't see how you can stand to listen to that stuff," Seth complained. "It's awful."

The three Kerrigan men sat talking for a while, and then Seth said, "Dad, I want you to know something."

"What's that, Seth?"

"I know it's hard on you trying to decide about what we all ought to do. We wish we could do something to help you with it . . ."

"I don't think anyone can help, son. Only the Lord."

Seth, however, seemed to have something else to say. "Well, I just want you to know, Dad—whatever you decide, it will be all right with me. If you do have to leave us with Aunt Minnie, we'll make the best of it. You won't be gone all that long. We just don't want you to worry about us."

"That's extra good of you to say so, son. I know Aunt Minnie is kindhearted, and she wants to be helpful. I also know that she's not the most cheerful person in the world, but—"

"I'll say she's not cheerful," Juan muttered. "She's like an accident going someplace to happen." He held up his hands quickly. "All right—all right. I'm sorry, Dad. Really, she's a pretty nice old lady. It's just that—well, I don't think she *likes* kids a lot."

"Pearl keeps praying that we can all stay together somehow," Seth said with a little smile. "She keeps saying that God can do it if He wants to."

"That's right," Juan put in. "Every day she says, 'Jesus can fix anything.'"

"Well, He can," Mr. Kerrigan said. "No question about that. And Pearl's a little child who trusts Jesus. He once said that older people should trust Him the way a little child does." Their dad smiled. "We'll just wait and see what the Lord will do. He'll do something, I'm sure."

"Hey, that's cool!" Juan shouted.

The four Kerrigan kids were gathered in the rec room and were making music together. Duffy was at the piano. Close by her was Pearl, seated at a set of drums. She looked very cute and very small sitting behind the drums. She seemed to have a natural rhythm, and she said she loved to bang them. "Back in Hong Kong," she would say, "we played gongs once in a while. And now I get to play these drums and cymbals. They're fun."

Duffy said, "You hit a sour note right in the middle of that last piece, Juan."

"No, I didn't, either. The rest of you were all off key," Juan protested in a loud voice. "I know when it happened, too, and I was right. The rest of you were all off key."

"You always say that." Seth frowned at him. "And you *were* off key."

"Well, whatever!" Juan said. *Whatever* was his favorite word this week. Everything was "whatever." He grinned cheerfully and said, "Let's do one of those Garth Brooks songs."

"No. Let's do one of the Steven Curtis Chapman things. And I'll sing," Seth said.

"OK," Duffy agreed. "That sounds good to me."

The next time they stopped playing, Juan said,

"You know what? Maybe we'll be famous when we grow up and do Christian concerts and stuff like that."

"That would be neat," Seth said. "Thousands of people coming out to listen to us and hear about Jesus. But we'll have to practice and get really good if we're going to do anything like that."

Juan must have suddenly decided it was about time for a joke. He said, "Did you hear about the man who read that smoking was bad for your health, so he gave up reading?"

The other three groaned, and even Pearl said, "You tell the awfulest jokes I ever heard, Juan."

After the four of them had played a little longer, their father stuck his head through the doorway. "Time for bed, everyone. I've been enjoying the concert. Thank you very much."

He came into the rec room, and they gathered around him. He put his arms around as many of them as he could, and each one prayed a brief prayer. It was something that their mother had insisted on. Prayer in the morning, prayer at noon, and prayer before bedtime, she had always said firmly. Now it was a part of their daily family life. No one even had to mention it. They just did it.

Pearl was the last to pray, and she said, "Thank You, Jesus, for fixing it somehow so we can all stay together. Amen."

"You really believe the Lord can, don't you,

Pearl?" Mr. Kerrigan gave her a special smile, and then he hugged her.

The girls went to their room, and the boys went to theirs. And after Pearl and Duffy had showered, they both climbed into bed.

Duffy lay awake for a while, thinking. She finally dropped off, but she did not sleep soundly for long.

Suddenly Pearl was yelling, "Duffy! Duffy, wake up!"

Duffy must have been totally asleep. She came out of it with a start, then groaned and grunted. "What is it, Pearl? Can't you be quiet and let me have a little sleep?"

"Duffy, Duffy, wake up! I've got something to tell you!" Pearl was out of bed and ripping back Duffy's cover. "Wake up!" she kept crying.

"I'm awake. I'm awake. What is it? What time is it, anyway?"

"I don't know, but I just had a dream I've got to tell you about."

Duffy groaned again and rubbed her eyes. "You want to tell me a dream in the middle of the night? Go back to sleep! Tell me in the morning."

"But it's important, Duffy," Pearl insisted.

Duffy sighed. "Oh, all right. Tell me. Go ahead. What was it? It looks like I'm not going to get any sleep anyway till you settle down."

"I dreamed that the whole family—you and

me and Juan and Seth and Dad—we were all together in a real strange place."

Duffy sighed again. "What kind of a strange
place?"

"I don't know. Just different."

"You must remember *something* about it."

"Well, you know how it is with dreams—
they're kind of fuzzy."

"Sure, but was it a good dream—or was it a
nightmare? Was it scary? What's so *important*?"

"I just was so happy that we were all together."

"Well, it was a nice dream, then. Not scary at
all. Go back to bed."

"But maybe it means something," Pearl bub-
bled on eagerly. "Maybe it means that Jesus is
telling us that somehow He is going to keep our
family together."

Duffy could not help laughing. "Which is exactly what you were thinking about before you
went to bed. You do have nice dreams, Pearl. Now
go back to sleep."

Duffy pulled up her covers. She heard Pearl go
back to her bed. Soon her little sister's breathing
was regular, but now Duffy could not go to sleep.
Maybe she had been more worried about the family being split up than she had admitted. She
tossed, and she turned.

She may have dropped off for one long stretch
or two, but mostly the night was spent in fits of
sleep. She thought over and over again about the

problems. For one thing, she dreaded Aunt Minnie's coming. She could not help it. Aunt Minnie just wasn't very comfortable with boys and girls. But what could they do? What did Jesus want them to do?

As she lay there, an idea began to grow. Duffy Kerrigan was an imaginative girl. All of the Kerrigan kids were imaginative, but Duffy's imagination was the greatest of all. She lay very still now, knowing that something was coming together in her mind. Finally, after a long time, it fitted together like the pieces of a jigsaw puzzle. When the last piece was in place, she knew at least what the family *might* do.

"Pearl, wake up!"

It was Pearl's turn to be awakened out of a sound sleep.

"What—what is it?" she muttered. "Is it morning?"

"It's almost morning. Get up. We got to go talk to the guys."

"About what?" Pearl came awake quickly then.

"It's about something that we maybe could do to keep the family together. Come on."

"Do you want to wake Dad up?"

"We'll talk to the guys first. That might be a better idea."

"Sure, we can talk to Dad later."

The two girls padded to the boys' room and tapped gently at their door.

The boys seemed to wake up slowly. Finally a

tousle-headed Juan opened the door. He was wearing white shorts and a loud purple shirt. He said crossly, "What are you doing up in the middle of the night? And what are you doing here?"

Then Seth appeared. He had on the bright red pajamas that he liked so much. They were so red they almost hurt Duffy's eyes.

"What's going on?" Seth asked. "Is something wrong? Is the house on fire?"

"No," Duffy said. "Nothing's wrong. Maybe something is right." She shoved her way past them into the room, followed by Pearl. Then she said, "Listen. Pearl had a dream."

"You came down to tell us Pearl's dream?" Juan groaned. "Couldn't that wait until morning?"

"No, it can't. Tell them your dream, Pearl," Duffy ordered.

The two boys listened as Pearl told her dream. Still, Juan just shrugged. "Well, that's nice, but it could have waited until morning."

"No, it couldn't. I couldn't go back to sleep. Her dream started me thinking. I kept thinking of us all together in some faraway place. What could we do to have the family together in a faraway place? So I've come up with a master plan. We won't need Aunt Minnie."

"A master plan. Well, that sounds important," Seth said. "What is it?"

"Sit down, and I'll tell you. Then we'll go tell Dad and see what he says."

4

A SCARY FAMILY MEETING

What in the world is going on?"

Mr. Kerrigan acted as if he'd been jerked out of a sound sleep by an avalanche. He struggled to a sitting position, rubbed his eyes, and peered like an owl at the four youngsters who had invaded his bedroom.

"We've got to talk to you about something important, Dad," Duffy announced. She switched on the light, and her father blinked and held his hands in front of his eyes. "I know this is a funny time but—"

"A funny time? I should say it's a funny time." Squinting at his wristwatch, their father gasped. "Why, it's four-thirty in the morning! It's not even daylight yet!"

"I know, Dad," Duffy said, "but we've got something really important to talk to you about."

He looked around at all their faces—first Duffy, then serious Seth, and grinning Juan, and the smallest, Pearl. When Pearl stepped close and touched him, the way she often did, he put his arm around her and sighed. "All right, then. What's all the excitement about?"

"Well, you see, Dad," Duffy began excitedly. "Pearl had this dream, and that made me think of something . . ." Brimming over with words, Duffy explained what had happened. She finished by saying, "And now I think maybe God has given us a master plan."

"Oh, a master plan, is it? Well, that's good. Nothing like a master plan to get the show on the road." Mr. Kerrigan tousled Juan's hair, which was already a mess, and gave Duffy a look. "And what is your master plan, Miss Duffy Anne Kerrigan?"

"Well, it's this. We all feel that the Lord really wants our family to stay together. Don't you feel that way, too, Dad?"

"He usually wants families together, yes. It's about to break my heart to think about leaving you while I go to the other side of the world. But how—"

"Let me tell, Dad," Duffy said, putting a finger on his lips. "You know we've all been praying about what to do—especially Pearl—and here's what we think the Lord wants us to do." Taking a deep breath, Duffy looked around for support from the other three. Then, seeing their approving faces, she said, "We've decided that the Lord would like us to go with you on your trips."

"That's totally impossible!"

"Nothing is impossible with God, Daddy. That's what the preacher said last Sunday. It's in the Bible." Pearl spoke firmly.

Mr. Kerrigan gave the little girl a squeeze and said, "I know that He is able to do anything He chooses to do. But at the same time, He wants us to use common sense."

Seth said in his short and clipped British accent, "Please listen to Duffy, Dad. I do think she's onto a very fine idea."

"I am," Duffy said. "It's a wonderful idea. Now, here's what we think we ought to do. This summer will be no problem, since school is out. But when school starts . . . well . . . we really don't want to stay here with Aunt Minnie. She's a nice lady and all but—"

"I know. 'She doesn't know anything about taking care of kids,'" Mr. Kerrigan said. "You've said all that before. But what about our problem? There's really no one else able to stay with you."

"Like I said, this summer there'll be no problem, Dad. We can all just go with you when you go to Africa."

"And then what? What about September?

What about when school's *not* out? You'd be absent so much that all of you would fail."

"That's my plan. We can go to school at home. People do that all the time."

Mr. Kerrigan stared at her. Then he said, "I know some families homeschool their children, and they do a fine job, but still . . ." He shook his head. "I'm not sure I'm qualified to do something like that, Duffy."

"You don't have to worry," Juan said quickly. "You have such smart children that all you'll have to do is give us some directions. We'll do all the work."

"That's right," Duffy said. She found herself getting even more excited. "You know my best friend, Marie. She goes to school at home. I'll bet her mom and dad would tell you how it works and what you have to do. We can get all the books and workbooks and take them with us. Wherever we go, we can do our schoolwork, and you can check it and give us assignments and tests and stuff."

"I think it's a great idea, Dad," Seth said. "You know Jimmy Oats. He's homeschooled, too, and he's won all kinds of awards. Jimmy's done all right getting taught at home. We will, too."

"Please, Daddy! We can do it!" Pearl pleaded.

The discussion went on for some time, while everyone sat on their father's bed.

It seemed to Duffy that he was bringing up every argument he could think of, but finally he just threw up his hands. "I don't know what else to say—except that I see big problems with this."

"Anyway, all of us have prayed about it, Dad," Duffy told him. "Now you can pray about it, too, and see what the Lord says."

"Yes, Daddy. You told us Jesus fixes things, and maybe this is His fixing," Pearl said.

The four youngsters watched their father's face. Duffy was still hoping and praying that he would agree. His decision meant a great deal to them all.

At last he sighed and nodded. "All right. I'll do this much. I promise to at least look into the idea. I'll pray about it, and I'll talk to Pastor Ryan about it."

"Hooray!" Juan yelled. "We're going to go to Africa!"

"Not so fast. I said I'd pray about it. Remember, God may still say no. The pastor may advise against it, and that would certainly make me slow to do this. We'll just have to wait and see."

Pastor Ryan was not only the pastor of the Kerrigans' church, but he was a close friend of the family as well. He sat in his study listening as Mr. Kerrigan poured out his problem. When Mr. Kerrigan seemed to be finished, he said, "And what do you think about it all, Jim?"

"Well, taking the children along and teaching them at home sounds good in a way. It would keep the family together—but it's such a big

41

undertaking. I don't know anything about home-schooling."

"I would say you can learn. The homeschool movement is a fine thing. It's a growing thing." The pastor nodded slowly. "Now, not every parent is qualified to teach his children, but I know you well. I believe you have teaching ability. And with children like yours, I think you could make a success of it."

"But this summer—what about hauling four kids to places in the middle of Africa? I'm told that we'll have to live in tents part of the time. The food will be local—whatever we can get. And what if they get sick?"

"All those things are true. I'm glad to hear you say the children have been praying about the decision. And you've prayed about it. Now I'm going to pray for direction for you. But on the whole, Jim, the idea looks workable to me. Let's both pray about this, and you come back and see me when you have an answer from God," Pastor Ryan said.

Mr. Kerrigan left the pastor's study, and for the rest of the day he kept to himself. He knew there were a hundred things to do if he was going to leave on time, but first he had to be sure the family was doing the right thing.

"Look, Duffy, it's very simple," Seth said patiently. "All you have to do to solve this problem is transpose these numbers."

The two were in the recreation room, where Seth was working out a math problem. Duffy watched his pencil fly over the paper. He was a genius at math, she thought. He liked math so well that he even worked out problems in the summertime, when he didn't have to—just for fun.

Duffy was not good at math at all. Sometimes she grew upset because she had such trouble with numbers. But, on the other hand, she knew she did some things much better than Seth did.

After watching him work for a while, she said, "Seth, I've been wondering about something. Pearl's dream is what got me thinking about going along with Dad and going to school at home. Do you think the Lord made Pearl dream that dream?"

Seth's dark features grew very serious. He always acted more grown up than the other Kerrigan children, and especially more so than Duffy. She knew she could be flighty at times. "Could be," he said. "The Lord talked to some of the Bible people that way."

"That's what I thought." Then she said, "What are we going to do if Dad says we can't go? Aunt Minnie will make all of us miserable."

"Whatever Dad decides," Seth said quickly, "we must not let him know we're disappointed. We just need to keep praying that the Lord will show him what he should do. I want us to stay together as much as you do. But Dad likes the kind of work he does—he wants to keep on taking pictures . . ."

"I know he does. I can't imagine him working in a store or doing anything but taking pictures and writing."

"Neither can I. We don't want him stuck in some job where he'll not be happy."

"You're trying to tell me something, aren't you, Seth?"

"Well, I think you already know it. We've got to be very careful, Duffy. If Dad decides that God really doesn't want us to go along on this trip, we must not complain about it. We must be very cheerful and tell him that we all love him anyway, and that we'll all pray for him. And if that's what he decides, then it's fine with us."

"That'll be hard for me. I want to go along so bad."

"So do I, Duffy. But we don't always get the things we want."

"I know you've all been wondering about what's going to happen. So now you're going to find out."

Duffy's father had rounded up all four of the Kerrigan kids and brought them into the dining room. They sat at the table where their father had placed them, and Duffy suddenly found that it was difficult to breathe. This was such a scary

44

family meeting. *He's going to tell us. And what if he says no?* she thought. *I don't think I could stand it.*

She looked at Juan. Maybe he was having similar thoughts. Duffy knew that Seth had talked to Juan very sternly, saying, "You must not show any disappointment if Dad decides we're to stay home. And don't complain about Aunt Minnie." Maybe right now he was preparing himself to grin even when he didn't feel like it.

Only Pearl looked happy. Duffy envied her.

But then her father was speaking. "I've talked to the pastor, and I've prayed about it, and here's what I think the Lord would have us do." He took a deep breath and said, "You're going to go with me on *this one trip*—"

Mr. Kerrigan could say no more. All four youngsters were shouting. Juan was doing a war dance around the dining room. Pearl jumped up and ran to her father. He grabbed her and held her and grinned broadly. Duffy came to his side also, and he put his other arm around her.

At last he said, "All right. Let's have a little order here," and finally they quieted down. "Here's what we will do, family. I'll take you on this one trip. Some things will be hard—you've probably got to have some shots, and I don't know what all else. We'll need passports. There's just a lot we'll have to do. And it's going to be tough to get it all done in a hurry."

"We can do it," Duffy cried. "We can do it, Dad!"

"I believe we can. But I want to make something perfectly clear. This is just a trial trip. If it doesn't work out—for any reason—then you'll just have to plan staying home and going to your regular school the next time I have to go overseas."

"And I know what that means," Juan said. "It means Aunt Minnie."

"That's right. It means Aunt Minnie. But that's the way it has to be. I believe this is what God wants us to do."

Seth was grinning. "I'm glad you decided that, Dad. But we had already talked it over, and whatever you said was going to be all right with us."

"And I'm glad you feel like that, son."

Juan grinned broadly. He seemed to have suddenly thought of something funny. He said, "Did you hear about the man that was accused of getting fired from every job he ever had?"

"No, I'm afraid I didn't," Mr. Kerrigan said with a sigh. "What about him?"

"He said, 'That proves I'm no quitter!'" Juan's white teeth flashed. "Whatever else we're going to be, we're not going to be quitters, Dad!"

5

A NEW
FRIEND

The flight attendant came down the aisle, smiling and checking the seat belts. She was small and pretty and had blonde hair and friendly bright blue eyes. When she reached the center of the plane, she stopped and looked at the passengers for a moment, then spoke to the tall, lean man in an aisle seat.

"Well," she asked with a smile, "are you taking a group of prizewinning scholars on a trip?"

All the Kerrigans were used to this. Duffy's father grinned and said, "Why, no. These are all my children. We're on our way to Africa."

The flight attendant just looked at them for a moment. And Duffy watched, knowing exactly what was on her mind. People always wondered the same thing. *How can these be your children?*

They're clearly all different nationalities. "Well, you certainly have a fine family. Your wife's not accompanying you this time?"

"No, she's not."

Perhaps the stewardess noticed the expression on Duffy's face. Or perhaps she noticed the way Seth and Pearl both lowered their heads. To cover up her mistake, she quickly added, "Well, I know you're going to have a fine time. It'll be an exciting experience for you in a brand-new and different place. And maybe a little scary?"

Now Juan looked up and grinned broadly. "But we take care of each other."

"You do? Why, that's real fine."

"Oh, sure," Juan said, his eyes sparkling. "One time my little sister here swallowed a cricket, and I took care of her."

"Oh my!" the flight attendant exclaimed. "Did you call the doctor?"

"No," Juan said innocently. "I just fed her some insect powder."

For a moment the stewardess was speechless. Then, when the other children began laughing at Juan's joke, she laughed too.

"Well, I'm the one who is going to take good care of you on this flight. You're going to get the best food and the best service of anybody on any airplane."

The trip proved to be an exciting adventure for all of the youngsters. Their father, of course, was accustomed to long plane rides. Seth had once flown from Africa, but he had been too young to remember that, so flying was a new experience for him too.

They had a wonderful lunch, just as the flight attendant had promised. Then, after they grew tired of looking down at the ocean, there was a movie to watch. It was a rather gross movie, Duffy thought, and almost right away Pearl said, "I don't want to watch this, Daddy."

"That's good judgment, Pearl," Mr. Kerrigan said. "Let's get out those games that we brought."

Their father had seen to it that part of their carry-on baggage included a game or two. He'd also said that there might be long days in Africa when the children would want something to do. So now they paired off. Juan and Seth played chess, and Pearl and Duffy started a game of checkers.

This is going to work out, Duffy thought. *Thank you, Lord, for showing us a way for all of us to stay together.*

The big plane came down with a thump at the Mombasa airport. As soon as a flight attendant said they could unbuckle their seat belts, the Kerrigan kids began scrambling to get up and off.

"There's no hurry," their father said. "No sense fighting the rush. Just sit back and let the plane empty a little. Then we can just stroll off."

They did what he said, but Duffy knew everybody was eager to see what Africa looked like.

"Do you suppose there'll be any lions in the airport?" Pearl asked timidly.

Mr. Kerrigan laughed. "I doubt it. You have to get out of the big city to see lions, I think. Well, let's get off now."

They disembarked, and as they walked down the stairs, Duffy looked around her. "It's not near as big as the airport in New York."

"Of course not, silly," Seth said. "Mombasa would fit into New York fifty times. It's just a small place. You might as well get used to that."

They had to go through customs. That took some time, because that was where people in uniforms checked through all their bags. Then they passed on into the main part of the airport with their luggage. Duffy was surprised and disappointed again.

"I thought there would be all these natives in loincloths and stuff like that," she said. "These people are dressed just like everybody else."

She kept looking around. She noticed that there were a few exceptions—here and there some were indeed wearing their tribal outfits. But most of the men were dressed in the kind of clothes she was used to seeing back home.

Her father told her, "Once we get out of Mombasa and into the country, then you'll see all the native things you want to."

The rest of the day, the youngsters just followed their father around. He found the family a hotel and began making plans for tomorrow. It was now late, so they could do little today. Then he showed them on a map where they would be going.

"Here's Africa," he said, pointing. "And you see this spot way over here on the eastern side? That's where the Masai people live."

"What country is it, Dad?" Juan asked.

"The Masai country is half in Kenya and half in Tanzania. We'll be going to a village in Tanzania."

Duffy looked closely at the map. She said, "I bet there aren't any good roads there—any superhighways or interstates or anything."

Her father chuckled. "You won't find much of that anywhere in Africa."

"How do we get to the village in Tanzania, Dad?" Seth asked.

"We'll rent us a Land Rover, and my editor has arranged for a guide for us. I've never met the man, but it ought to be interesting."

"What tribe is he? Is he a Masai?" Seth asked with interest.

"Yes, he's a Masai warrior—and best of all, he is a Christian, I understand. I'm glad for that. We'll need all the help we can get finding our way around Africa. And the Lord has given us one of His own children to help us."

"He'll keep us from being eaten by lions, won't he?" Pearl said confidently.

"That he will, sweetheart. That he will!"

The next day the Kerrigans scurried around Mombasa and got a great deal done in preparation for their trip. Mr. Kerrigan rented a Land Rover and a huge trailer to carry their equipment. They bought two big tents and all sorts of camping gear, including cots and cookware. They loaded in the trailer all of the canned foods that they might need, along with dried food that could be easily prepared at a campsite. They even bought some clothes—mostly shorts and lightweight shirts. And each of them bought a helmet to keep off the burning sun.

"It's really *hot* out here," Juan said.

"Sure it is. We're close to the equator, and the equator's closer to the sun than we are in our part of America," Seth said importantly. He had become quite an authority on Africa. He had read some library books about it before they left home.

"When are we leaving, Dad?" Pearl asked that night after they had their family prayer time.

"First thing in the morning. We'll go to a little village outside of Mombasa, and there we'll meet our guide."

The family got up at dawn and left Mombasa. Mr. Kerrigan drove the Land Rover, pulling the heavily loaded trailer. The road turned out to be better than anybody had expected, but he said,

"This won't last long. We'll be going on what looks like a goat track before we're through."

Then they arrived at the little village where they were to pick up their guide. They stopped at the small store where they were supposed to meet, and Mr. Kerrigan was disappointed to find that the man was not there.

"Maybe he forgot," Duffy said. "Or maybe he just hasn't got here yet. I read that people don't pay much attention to time in Africa."

"That's pretty well true," her dad said. "The people don't live by their watches the way we do. That's because, remember, most of them don't have any watches."

They stood around and waited all morning long, and still he did not come. Finally they bought some lunch. They were sitting out under an awning, still waiting, when suddenly Pearl said, "Look down the street. Maybe that's him coming right now."

Everybody turned to look at the man who was walking up the main street of the village toward them. He was one of the most unusual looking human beings Duffy had ever seen. He was well over six feet tall and very thin. He looked strong, though, and in his hand he carried a steel-tipped spear. He wore a single red garment draped over one shoulder and tied under the armpit on the other side. He was barefooted. Actually, Duffy thought, he was a very handsome man.

"Look at his hair. It's all red," Juan said.

"I know about that," Seth said. "That's what they call *ochre*. It's kind of a mineral. They put it on their hair and then do their hair in little braids."

The guide came closer. Sure enough, his reddish hair was in plaits, and it hung down his back. His legs were also coated with the same ochre and were striped like a zebra. It was a light-colored ochre and looked as if someone had made patterns by drawing his fingertips through it, exposing the dark skin. That was what made the stripes.

Duffy saw that he wore colorful beads and buttons and metal objects to adorn his long earlobes. He wore a neckband too, which she would later find out was made from the stomach lining of a goat.

The Kerrigan kids and their father all got up to greet him.

Then the man was standing before them, and he grinned broadly. "My name is Naikosiai, but you may call me Naiko."

"I'm Jim Kerrigan, Naiko, and these are my children. This is Duffy, Seth, Juan, and Pearl."

Naiko closely looked at each one. Then he gave a nod and turned back to their father. "God has given you a fine family. You will never get them mixed up—they are all so different."

"That's right." Mr. Kerrigan grinned, too.

"We're glad to see you, Naiko. I wouldn't want to make this trip without a good guide."

"Maybe Jesus God Himself has sent me to help you," Naiko said.

"I'm sure He has. As I say, we do need help. Are you ready to start, then?"

"Yes."

Naiko seemed fascinated with the Land Rover and with the mountain of supplies in the trailer. He laughed and said, "You will not starve to death, that is certain."

They all got into the Land Rover then and, following Naiko's directions, began their journey toward the heart of Tanzania. They left the small village behind, and soon the road began to narrow. It was not paved any longer. The country stretched out ahead of them, and Duffy was sure she could see for miles and miles.

"This is beautiful country," Mr. Kerrigan said to Naiko, who was sitting upright beside him.

"I would like to see your homeland someday," Naiko said. "It looks nothing like this, does it?"

"Not a bit. But then, most countries are different."

They drove and drove, then stopped to eat a snack of sandwiches.

Naiko accepted one of them and looked at it suspiciously. But when he tasted the sandwich, he nodded his approval. "It is good. What is it?"

"Peanut butter and jelly," Juan told him. "Do you like it?"

"If I cannot get regular food, I take what I can get. I'm always grateful for food to the good God."

"What do you like to eat most?"

"We Masai live by our herds, and from the cattle we get two good things, milk and blood."

In the backseat, Duffy had been in the midst of swallowing a bite of sticky sandwich. When she heard him say "blood," she began to cough. She had to take several swallows of bottled soda to clear her throat. She stared at the Masai sitting beside her father and asked weakly, "Did you say blood? To eat?"

"You must have to kill a lot of cows to get blood, then," Juan said.

Naiko looked back at him. "We do not kill them. We make a little puncture in their necks. We catch the blood from that, then close it up with cow dung. Then we put the blood in the milk, and we drink it."

Duffy made a bad mistake then. "That sounds *awful!* I would never drink anything like that!"

Her father frowned at her in the rearview mirror and said, "Duffy, you're going to find out that the customs are different here. Every country has its own special way of doing things."

But Duffy was truly horrified. "I don't see how you can do that."

Naiko looked back at her. He had a thin nose

and piercing dark brown eyes that had a kindly look. When he smiled—which he did then—he was really a fine-looking man. "I hope you will not be offended by some of my people's ways. Before I became a believer in Jesus, it was hard for me to accept the ways of the white man. And it may be hard for you to learn the ways of my people."

"We can do it," Seth said with a smile.

"Yes, we can," Juan agreed. And he grinned.

"Yes, we can," Pearl echoed.

Then Naiko said, "We will get to the village tomorrow. Tonight we will camp out."

"Well, that part will be fun!" Duffy said.

Again, Naiko smiled at her. "It will be a little different from camping out in your backyard in America."

THE
ROUGH GAME

The Kerrigans stopped early enough to put up their tents, and that took longer than Duffy thought it would. The kids slept in one tent, while Mr. Kerrigan and Naiko stayed in the other. They put mosquito netting over the entrances to the tents to keep the insects out, but it did not work perfectly. All four Kerrigan kids spent a great deal of time just slapping at mosquitoes and other bugs. The night was quite exciting, Duffy thought.

Sometime in the middle of the night, a loud sound awakened her. Everybody sat bolt upright, and Pearl cried out, "What's that? It sounds like a lion."

Then Naiko suddenly appeared at their tent door. Duffy could see his face gleaming in the bright moonlight. "That was a lion," he said, "but he will not harm you. He is far away."

"He sounds like he's just outside the tent!" Duffy said in a quavering voice.

"No, no, he is far away. He just sounds close. Do not fear. The Lord God will protect us," Naiko said. "Sleep now. It will soon be dawn."

Their dad woke them while it was still dark. But by the time the kids were up and had their faces washed, dawn was breaking. They then cooked a quick breakfast of eggs and fried beef over the campfire.

When it was time to eat, Naiko joined them. He tasted the eggs and said, "Good. I like eggs."

Mr. Kerrigan looked quickly at Duffy as if to make sure she made no remark about the eating habits of the Masai. He seemed to be relieved when she did not.

It took some time to clean up after breakfast, take down the tents, and pack everything. The sun was well on its way up when they left. Then they drove for hours, not stopping until noon.

Once Naiko said, "Look."

And they all looked in the direction in which he pointed. It was a huge herd of animals, and Pearl called out, "Oh, are they cows?"

"No. Not cows. They are wildebeests," Naiko said. "Wildebeests are the favorite food of the lion."

Duffy kept watching for lions. They did not

see any lions that afternoon, but once in the far distance they saw a herd of huge, lumpy animals.

"Elephants," Naiko told them.

They arrived at their village late in the afternoon. And the place turned out to be not at all what Duffy—or anyone else, for that matter—had expected. Most of the kids had seen movies about Africa, and they were expecting grass huts. Instead they found that the Masai settlement was quite different.

"Are those the houses? Where they live?" Duffy asked.

"Yes, this is what we call an *engang*. It is what you would call a village."

The *engang* was spread out over a large area, and it was made up of fenced sections, a little like yards. The fences were built of sharpened poles and saplings. The houses were odd, though. They looked like large loaves of bread, and they were the color of the earth. Around each one of them were many, many children playing.

Farther out, the Masai cattle were everywhere. The animals had long horns, and they were huge. Young boys, each dressed in a single reddish garment, watched them.

"Why do they stand like that?" Pearl asked. She was watching the boys. They stood on one leg. The sole of one foot rested on the knee of the supporting leg. They held their balance by leaning on a staff.

"It is the way of our people," Naiko said. "We all stand like that at times." Then he looked over at Duffy and grinned. "Do you think you could stand like that, little one?"

"I guess I could if I wanted to," Duffy said grumpily.

They moved on into the *engang,* and Naiko took them to meet some of the elders of the village. Most of them were very tall men. Some were young and strong looking. Others were gray-haired and bent over with age.

Naiko explained to the men in their language, which was called *Maa,* that the Kerrigan family would be visitors in the village. Then he listened while an ancient man with almost snow-white hair made a long speech.

He turned to Mr. Kerrigan and explained. "This is Meremo, a very important elder. He says he welcomes you to their homes and will do what he can to make you happy."

Duffy's dad nodded and made a short speech himself, thanking Meremo. Then he turned back to Naiko. "If you could take us to some place where we'll be out of the way, we'll set up our tents."

"I will show you a good place."

The place that Naiko led them to was an open area, and the sun was beating down on it. "This will be a good place," he said. "No one will bother you here."

"What about lions?" Duffy asked suspiciously.

"They usually do not come into the village. A leopard will occasionally come, but we will trust the good Lord that you will be safe."

Having already had some practice setting up the tents, the family soon had them both erected this time. It took a while to organize everything, though. Mr. Kerrigan had brought along a great deal of equipment for doing his work. He set up a folding desk, and he stored his photographic supplies in a cabinet.

"Why don't you take a look around the village while I'm getting things organized, kids?" he said. "You might as well get used to the place. It'll be home for a while."

"I will be your guide," Naiko said.

He led them away from the tents, and as he did he explained a little of the Masai way of life. "The life of a Masai warrior has three parts: boyhood, warriorhood, and elderhood. The warriors," he said, "are divided into junior and senior warriors. About every fifteen years, a new group of warriors comes of age. Then we have great ceremonies."

As they walked back through the *engang,* Duffy again noticed the many boys and girls. Also, more than once, she saw a man pick up a child and hug it or kiss it or play with it.

"The Masai men love children, don't they?" she said.

"Yes, they do. All Masai love children very much. Sometimes you will hear a parent calling a child 'My Fragile Bones' or 'Child of My Beloved Man.' All Masai babies are well cared for. And they are never lost—whoever is close when one gets in trouble immediately becomes its father or the mother. Listen to that mother over there. She is singing to her baby."

The Kerrigan kids stopped and watched a Masai woman who was holding a fat, pudgy baby. The woman had beaded ornaments in her ears and around her neck. The baby wore a single garment. It had beads on it, too.

"What does the song say, Naiko?" Seth asked.

"It says:

> Grow up, my child,
> Grow up like a mountain.
> Equal Mount Naru,
> Equal Mount Kenya,
> Equal Kilimanjaro.
> Help your mother and father."

Then Naiko said, "Later, she will sing another song. It is one that I learned when I was only a baby. All mothers sing it:

Walk, walk, walk, my little one.
Let us walk, my little one.
Slowly, let us walk slowly."

Duffy was fascinated by the way that the women cared for their babies and by the affection that the fathers had for them.

"It's not always that way in our country," Seth said quietly to her. "I think the Masai are better fathers and mothers than some of our people are."

They passed by more boys and girls and young people. They seemed to be playing games.

"What are the games they play?" Juan asked with interest.

"The boys there are making little kraals out of the earth. The word *kraal* sometimes means the village. But a kraal is also a place where we keep the cattle. The boys put pebbles or berries inside them to be the sheep and the cattle. Little girls play with dolls made from mud. They play with jacks made from stones or berries. Sometimes—see that group over there?—they play hide and seek. And all children like to play that they are grown-ups."

Pearl said suddenly, "All of the littlest children have their teeth gone!"

"That's true." Naiko nodded his head. "When a child is four or five years old, an experienced elder woman removes the two lower front teeth. That makes the child beautiful. It also makes it possible to feed the child through the small opening if it gets sick and is not able to open its mouth."

"What about when the new teeth grow in?" Duffy asked.

"Then they are removed again."

"Does everybody have their ears pierced here?"

"Men and women both do. Between seven and eight years, both boys and girls have the upper part of their right ear pierced. When that is healed, the left ear is pierced, too. In a year or two, a bigger hole is pierced in both earlobes. We stick wooden plugs or wads of leaves into the holes. You see," he said, "the larger the earlobe, the more beautiful the person is."

"I guess we're pretty ugly, then," Juan said, and he laughed. "I don't have any ears pierced at all."

"I do," Duffy said, "but they're so tiny."

"Maybe we could start today," Naiko said with a straight face. "I will pierce your ears for you. All of you."

A howl of protest went up from all the Kerrigans, and the Masai chuckled. "No, that is not your way. It is the Masai way."

Duffy thought they had a wonderful time exploring the village. Pretty soon they saw a group of boys and girls about Seth's age playing some sort of game with a ball.

"Now," Naiko said, "it is time you meet some of our young people. Many of these can speak English."

He walked up to the group and said, "Simel, these are our new friends." He told the ballplayers the Kerrigans' names.

The boy Simel, who appeared to be about twelve, looked at them all and asked, "Would you like to play?"

"Sure," Juan said. "What are the rules?"

"We have no rules. We just hit the ball."

"How do you keep score?" Juan wanted to know.

"What is *score?* We just hit the ball."

A girl about Duffy's age came up beside Simel.

"Hello," Duffy said. "My name is Duffy."

"I am Karimi. I am Simel's sister. Naiko is our uncle."

"That's right," Naiko said. "And these visitors are very important people. Now, let the game begin. You boys can play, but it would be a rough game for girls. Especially for you, my Pearl."

But Duffy instantly said, "I want to play, too."

"You might get hurt," Simel warned. "You're too little."

"Oh, let her play," Karimi said. "You let me play all the time."

"You are a Masai girl. She is not."

Of course, this made Duffy all the more determined.

At last Simel gave in. "All right. You can play."

Duffy had played on a soccer team for several years and thought she could keep up with anyone. Before long, she found out differently. The

Masai boys and girls were quick and strong, and she was soon panting for breath. She was determined not to show it, however. She was going to keep up as best she could.

Pearl stood at the side, watching the ball game. The game was simple enough, but it was indeed rough. The boys and girls kept fighting over a leather ball that was stuffed with grass.

As she watched, the ball came close to Duffy. She started for it, but suddenly she was struck in the stomach by Simel, who was making a grab for it at the same time. Pearl could see that what happened was not intentional, but it knocked Duffy backward, and she seemed unable to draw her breath for a moment.

Pearl hurried over to her, and so did Simel. "Are you all right?" Pearl asked anxiously.

Struggling to breathe and red-faced, Duffy got to her feet. "You did that on purpose, Simel!"

Simel just grinned at her. "It is a game. We all get hit and fall down sometimes."

Now Karimi ran up. "That is true," she said. "Sometimes the older boys play in the middle of the cattle, where they get stepped on by the big cows."

But Duffy turned around and stalked away.

"You shouldn't have treated a guest that way," Karimi said to Simel.

"It was an accident! And she was the one that

wanted to play," Simel said. "I told her it was a hard game."

Then Karimi turned to Pearl. "Your sister is not hurt, is she?"

"She isn't hurt. And she shouldn't have been so prideful. We all know it was just an accident."

Karimi seemed to want to stop playing ball and just talk. "Tell me about your family and where you come from," she said.

It turned out that the two girls spent the rest of the afternoon together and were fast friends by the time the sun went down. When they were about to part for the evening, Pearl said, "Duffy gets her feelings hurt easy. She'll just have to learn."

"Does she learn easy?"

"Well, no. I'm afraid she doesn't."

"That is too bad. We all have to learn."

'Yes, but Duffy is very proud in some ways."

"We Masai are proud, but we have to learn how to humble ourselves."

"I think everybody does," Pearl said. "The Bible talks a lot about being humble."

"I do not know the Bible, but our elders teach us that no man or woman is strong enough to stand alone."

"I know that, but Duffy doesn't—not yet."

"She must learn, then." Karimi nodded wisely. "Sooner or later, she will have to learn."

Pearl suddenly said, "Karimi, you don't seem

strange to me at all. You're just like one of my friends at home."

"Perhaps that is because you are not a born American."

"Maybe. But anyway, I had to learn not to pick my friends by what they look like. Or where they come from, either."

Karimi smiled. "That is good."

"And now all we have to do is try to make Duffy see that—that people have to be judged on what they are—not what they look like."

THE MASAI
WEDDING

Again the mosquitoes got into the tent where the Kerrigan kids slept, but they resigned themselves to it. "I guess we just got to be tougher than mosquitoes," Juan said the next morning at breakfast.

They had all decided to help with the cooking, and Juan had volunteered to make pancakes today. The smell of the frying meat that would accompany them was in the air.

Duffy thought she was about to starve. She looked at Juan, who was standing over the fry pan, and said, "Will the pancakes be long?"

He laughed. "No. They'll be *round*—just like they always are. Who wants a long pancake?"

Duffy groaned. "You've got to tell those corny *jokes!* Why can't you just say yes or no?"

When breakfast was almost ready, Simel and Karimi appeared. They seemed hesitant to approach at first, but Seth called out quickly, "Come and join us! There's plenty to eat!"

The two came forward rather bashfully, but they were greeted warmly. Then Pearl put pancakes on two plates and handed them to the visitors. "Try these," she said. "We eat them with syrup on them. But we have honey, too."

Simel looked at the knife and fork. Then he picked up the pancake with his fingers and rolled it up. He took a bite but did not comment.

"Do you like it?" Duffy asked.

"Yes. It's all right."

Karimi was more enthusiastic. "It is *very* good!" she said.

For someone who did not seem to care for American pancakes, Simel did all right, however. He ate three of them.

And then Duffy made a mistake. She said, "Now, isn't that better than eating blood?"

"Duffy!" Seth sounded horrified.

Her father sent her a disapproving frown and shook his head.

"What do you eat in your home where you come from?" Simel asked. He clearly did not like what Duffy had said. Perhaps he thought she was making fun of his way of life.

"We eat awful stuff," Juan said cheerfully. "Some people eat snails."

"Juan! That's the French people that eat snails," Duffy protested.

"Well, we eat some pretty bad stuff. You'll have to admit it. Look at all that gooey stuff that they sell at the supermarkets."

"I never noticed you turning any of it down!" Duffy exclaimed.

Simel listened to Juan describe some of the sugary confections available in food markets in the United States. Then he said, "We wouldn't feed that to our dogs."

While the others were talking, Duffy's father managed to whisper, "Duffy, please don't say anything else about the way the Masai live. *Please*."

Duffy knew she was wrong, but she was stubborn, and she refused to apologize.

When they had finished breakfast, Mr. Kerrigan said, "I'm going to start taking pictures today."

"Can I go with you, Dad?" Seth asked.

"Sure, son. Let's go."

Seth and his father took off while the girls started to clean up the dishes, and Mr. Kerrigan took many pictures in the village. "I just hope I brought enough film," he said. "I have to take a lot more pictures than I need, just to be sure of getting good ones. For every hundred pictures I take, maybe one will be good enough to use."

They moved here and there around the *engang* all morning. And then Seth said, "Oh, look, Dad.

There's Juan playing with Simel, and Pearl's playing with Karimi."

"I wonder why Duffy's not with them," Mr. Kerrigan said.

"Aw, Dad, you know how she is. She's stubborn. And she keeps saying things about the way the Masai people do things—like eating blood—and that hurts Simel's feelings."

"I know. Duffy is a little thoughtless. I'll have a talk with her about this sort of thing."

"I think you should," Seth said in his British voice. "She needs it."

The next few days were delightful for all the Kerrigan kids. They learned a great deal about Africa. They saw giraffes and zebras and many other animals they had seen only at the zoo. And they actually caught a glimpse of a lion.

It was on the fourth day of their visit, one morning at breakfast, that Naiko turned to Duffy and Pearl and said, "You will like what is going to happen in our *engang* today."

"Won't *we* like it?" Juan asked. "Or is it just for girls?"

"I hope you will all like it. It is a wedding."

"Oh, good!" Pearl's eyes sparkled. "I like weddings. Who's getting married?"

"The sister of Simel and Karimi. Her name is Lotoon."

"I'll have to get some pictures of that—if it will be all right," Mr. Kerrigan said.

"I am sure it will," Naiko told him.

Later in the day, as they made their way toward the spot where the marriage would be held, Naiko explained, "This match was planned by the bride's and groom's families long before the children were even born."

"Well, I think that's awful!" Duffy exclaimed loudly. "They may not even like each other when they grow up."

"It is different in your country. But does your way always make marriage work out well there?"

Duffy did not answer. She knew that, many times, marriages in the United States were not happy marriages.

"I just wish you would stop criticizing the way these people live," Seth grumbled when Naiko moved away. "You're not doing us any good."

The wedding was very interesting. The best man and the bride's family were all covered with ochre and dressed in their tribal finery. All necklaces were polished, and beautiful, soft, beaded skins had been prepared for the bride to wear. The bride's mother had dressed her in them.

There were many ceremonies, and then Naiko said, "Watch what happens now."

The wedding was in the tribal language, and the Kerrigans could not understand what the bride was saying, but Duffy thought she seemed very unhappy.

"She is not *really* unhappy," Naiko explained, "but she must show sorrow for leaving her home. And when they leave, you will notice that she does not look back. She is forbidden to look back."

"Why is that?" Pearl asked.

"For fear she might turn to stone from grief."

"Your people really believe that?" Duffy asked.

"Not really. It is just one of the stories that are in our history."

They watched the bride leave, escorted by the women of her family. She was blessed by her father with milk from a gourd. And the best man went before the group, removing any obstacles in the bride's path. She was carrying a white walking stick, and she kept looking at the ground. When they reached their destination—the new husband's home—many children were there to greet them and bow their heads respectfully.

"I wonder if he'll pick her up and carry her over the threshold," Pearl whispered.

"I don't think so," Duffy whispered back. "I think that only happens in America."

Indeed, the tall bridegroom did not carry his bride through the doorway. But there were many wedding gifts for the new couple. Mostly these were milk and meat and honey beer.

And after all this came a happy time of singing and dancing.

The men began to do something then that none of the Kerrigans had ever seen. First, they began to leap upward. Higher and higher their jumping went. Usually one at a time jumped, while the others cheered him on. But sometimes several leaped at once.

"Why, they just seem to float!" Juan exclaimed. "Look how high they can go."

"They'd make great basketball players. It looks like gravity doesn't have any effect on them," Duffy said.

The tall warriors, muscular and strong but lean, kept leaping high into the air. Often they would give their shoulders a twitch when they reached the peak of their leap. The women danced also, but theirs was a different kind of dance. They simply moved around gracefully.

The wedding celebration was a fine time—until Duffy managed to make one more mistake. When Naiko mentioned that the groom already had two wives, she cried, "Two wives! That's terrible! A man should only have one wife!"

"That is the Christian way," Naiko said quietly. "But my people have not yet accepted the Bible."

"Duffy, keep quiet!" her father muttered fiercely. "Quit criticizing the way these people do things. They are not believers in Jesus yet."

"That is true," Naiko said. "But they will soon come to know better how to live, now that some of us know Jesus. Just now they still love their old ways. I once did, too. It will take more than a day to stop these practices." He had a sad look in his eyes. Then he said, "You see, Jesus must be in their hearts first. *Then* they will change."

For some reason, Duffy was beginning to feel terrible about what she had said.

Naiko laid his hand on her shoulder. "Be kind in your thoughts to those who are different," he said. Then the big Masai turned and walked away.

A SURPRISE
HOUSE BUILDER

The Kerrigan kids loved Africa! Every morning they got up with excitement, for there was always something new and different for them to see. The Masai people, they soon found out, were wonderfully warmhearted, and the Kerrigans quickly grew very fond of them. They especially liked Simel and Karimi, who had become their constant companions. Simel had to spend much of his day herding the family's cattle, but Karimi had more time to be with them.

Their father said he was very happy with the way his project was turning out. "I'm going to have the best article on Africa ever written—and the best pictures too!" he declared with a grin.

"Sure you will, Dad." Seth grinned happily,

too, and his white teeth gleamed. "This is a wonderful place."

"I know it's not all been easy. It's like camping out all the time instead of living in a house. Don't you mind that, Seth?"

"No, I don't mind. And Juan doesn't mind. I'm surprised at how well Pearl and Duffy are taking it, though—with no indoor bathroom and having to take a bath in the river when you can. But Duffy . . . Dad . . . well, the Masai kids just don't seem to like her as much as they do Pearl."

"I know. And I'm getting a little worried about that." His father seemed to be thinking out loud. "I wish Duffy would just give up on trying to improve everybody she sees. The best thing we can do here is to show these people the loving concern of Jesus—not go tearing into telling them where they are wrong about things."

"But, Dad," Duffy protested, "look how these women have to work! Look over there right now at that poor woman. She's carrying a *huge* load of sticks."

Her father looked over to where a young Masai woman was, indeed, carrying a heavy load of firewood.

"Why can't the men do that hard work?"

"It's the Masai custom, Duffy. What she's doing is what her mother did and what her grandmother did," her dad said. "The women do that kind of work here. The men do other things."

"They go hunting and have fun, that's what. And the women do all the hard work."

"The men have to take care of all the cattle, Duffy. That's their main job. These people live for their cattle, and they have to have cattle to live. They even love grass, because it feeds the cattle."

Duffy knew all that was indeed true. She had watched the men as new calves were born, and there was a celebration almost as if it were a human child. The cattle were treated with great respect. They were all named, all had their own special brand, and the young boys watched over them very carefully.

"I know they love their cattle, and I know the men take care of them. But the women have such a hard life."

"The Masai people have their ways, Duffy, just as the American people have their ways. One thing you can say about them, though—they love their children."

"Yes, they do that," Duffy agreed. "I just wish that the women didn't have to work so hard."

Later that afternoon Pearl and Karimi came looking for Duffy. "Come with us," Pearl said. "We're going to help Tajewi build her house. She's another new bride."

"What's all this about building a house?" Duffy asked.

Pearl explained. "I found out all about it. Here in Masai country, the first thing a married woman has to do is to build her house."

"But the men are supposed to build the houses!" Duffy complained.

"No, that is not our way," Karimi said.

"And we're going to help her build it, Duffy. Come on—and don't say anything about how terrible it is for her having to build her own house!" Pearl whispered fiercely.

The three girls walked to where the new bride was busy putting up her own house. She seemed to have already made great progress.

Karimi introduced Pearl and Duffy. Tajewi spoke no English at all, but Karimi interpreted and then showed them Tajewi's house.

"The way we build our houses is to first stick long tree branches into the ground. Then we weave them together with smaller branches. As soon as the sticks are all in place, we plaster them over with mud along with leaves and grass."

The two girls watched with interest, and Duffy was very impressed.

"A woman can make a house any way she wants it," Karimi said. "They all have the same shape, but then we decorate them inside and outside."

"What's that stuff she's putting all over the framework?" Duffy asked.

"Oh, that's cow dung."

Duffy and Pearl gave each other shocked looks, but Karimi said, "It dries hard and turns away the rain. And we always have plenty of cow dung to use. When it rains, we patch any leaks with fresh dung."

Duffy managed to say nothing bad about that strange custom. Then she threw herself into helping put the outer coating on the house.

The girls stayed all day long. As they worked, Duffy thought they got to know the new bride quite well, even though she could not speak any English.

That night at their family Bible reading time, Duffy said, "We need to pray for Tajewi. She has to build her own house. That's terrible!"

"That's the way they do here," Juan said. "It's just the Masai people's custom. You ought to learn not to fuss about other people's customs."

Duffy snapped, "I still think it's a man's place to do some things!"

They had prayer time then. They prayed for their new friends here in Africa. They prayed for friends back home in the United States. And they prayed for the Lord's protection.

It was Pearl who prayed, "And, Lord, help us to understand these people who are so different from us. We know You want them to be Your children, Lord. And I pray that lots of them will let Jesus into their hearts."

A VISIT
WITH MEREMO

Juan, Seth, and Pearl had gotten used to the ways of the Masai people without any difficulty, their father thought. Perhaps it was because they came from foreign countries themselves rather than from America. In any case, Duffy seemed to be the only one of the four who had any problem.

"I can't understand it," Mr. Kerrigan said to Naiko one day. "Back home in the United States, Duffy was the sweetest child you can imagine. She was always bright and sunny. But she's changed since we got here. She's sullen, and she pouts, and I don't understand it."

"Some people have more trouble adjusting to the ways of foreigners than others do," Naiko said. The two were watching a herd of cattle file by. Naiko stood on one foot with the sole of his right foot resting on his other knee. He looked like a long crane as he leaned on his staff. Then he put his attention on his friend. "She will be all right. It will just take her a little more time."

Duffy felt angry with herself, but somehow she could not find a way to stop behaving so badly. She wanted to go to every member of her family and apologize. She wanted to go to those Masai people that she had come to know and apologize to them. But she found there was a stubbornness in her, and she simply could not do it.

It was a Thursday afternoon, and she had been out walking by herself. She saw Pearl, Juan, and Seth engaged in a game on the edge of the *engang,* and she hoped that one of them would ask her to join them. As it happened, nobody seemed to notice her, so Duffy walked on by, and her feelings were hurt even more.

"Good day to you."

Duffy looked up quickly to see Meremo, one of the elders of the *engang.* He was standing in the shade of a strangely shaped tree, and his old eyes were fixed on her. "Come and stand in the shade, daughter."

Glad for company, Duffy walked toward him. "You speak English very well, sir."

"Yes, my father worked with the white man for some years in Mombasa. I spent much time there."

"I wish I could speak your language as well as you speak English."

"It would take a long time, I'm afraid. It took me a long time to learn your language." He smiled. Then his old eyes studied her, and he said, "And what do you think of us by now, daughter?"

Duffy wanted to be truthful, but she hardly knew what to say. Then she said, "I like some of your ways very much. I like the way all of your people love children and care for them."

"Do not your people care for children?" The old man seemed highly surprised.

"Yes, they do. Most of the time they do. But not always," she said.

"Among our people also there are some who are not so loving," he told her. He then looked out over the herds of cattle that were grazing and said, "Our lives are very much tied to our cattle. That is all we know. All of our plans are dependent upon the cattle."

"And you do love your cattle too, don't you?"

"Oh yes. Our families know their own cattle and truly love them as one loves one's child. We've learned to recognize the voices of our animals. Every Masai is taught how to sing to them. And all know how to describe their horn formation, and their humps, and their colors . . ."

He went on speaking about how the Masai depended upon cattle almost entirely, and Duffy politely listened. The people drank the milk fresh or in a sour yogurt form, he said. Babies were fed ghee, which was something like butter. She learned that they slaughtered an animal only on certain occasions—such as when a person was sick or when the warriors were having a special time. Also, there seemed to be not much selfishness among the Masai. She could tell that.

"And we Masai love grass, because the cattle feed on it," Meremo told her. "If there is no rain, the women fasten grass onto their clothes and go to offer prayer to God that the rain might fall."

"Your people believe in God, then, Meremo?"

The Masai's wise old eyes looked at her. "The Masai believe in one god, *Engai,* who dwells on earth and in heaven. He is the supreme God, and no one else can be called by that name."

Duffy listened closely to all he told her, for she was very interested in perhaps being a missionary someday. Already her fertile mind was seeing herself grown up and coming back as a missionary to the Masai people.

"What do you pray most about, Meremo?"

"For children and cattle. When we meet one another we say, *'Keserian ingera? Keserian ingishu?'*"

"What is that?"

"It means, 'How are the children? How are the cattle?'"

"Do you know about Jesus?"

"Oh yes. The missionaries come sometimes. They will be here in three days."

"You are a Christian, then?"

"No, I am not. But some of my people are. Like Naiko. Some people were afraid he would be drawn away from us by being a Christian. But he has become a better man since following the Jesus God."

At that moment an excited voice rang out. "Duffy, Duffy, come quick! We're going to see a herd of zebra. A big herd." It was Juan, running toward them.

Duffy turned and bowed politely, as she had seen the Masai do many times. "Thank you, Meremo, for talking with me. What you said about your people was very interesting."

"We must speak again, daughter."

Some missionaries did come three days later, just as Meremo had said. There were two—an older man and his wife. Their names were Lois and Charles Simpson. They had been missionaries in Africa for many years, they said, and they seemed to speak the language well. They also seemed happy to meet all the Kerrigans and acted pleased when they came to the preaching service.

The service, Duffy thought, was certainly different from any church service she had seen in the States. A crowd of Masai came and listened, but no one sat down. All just stood around the missionary, who preached to them in their own language. Since the Kerrigans did not understand a word of it, Duffy did not know whether the sermon was good or not.

After the preaching was over and the people were dismissed, Mr. Simpson came over to the Kerrigan family to say good-bye. "We must be on our way to another village," he said.

"Did you ask if any of them wanted to become Christians?" Duffy asked him.

"I always do. I've been coming to this village now for six years. In that time, only three people —including your friend Naiko—have been saved. It is a hard place, but Jesus will be the victor. We must just be patient."

After the missionaries had gone, Duffy for some reason felt sad. She was standing beside a kraal— one of the enclosures that held the cattle—just watching the animals, when Naiko came by. He stopped and stood on one leg, as he always did, and talked for a while.

When the Masai finally walked on, Duffy began to pray. *Lord,* she began silently, *I haven't shown enough love to these people. I've been critical, and I want You to make me different. Give me a love for the Masai people. Help me to just let You change them the way You want to and when You want to.*

After she had prayed, Duffy found that she felt better. She got up and went to find Pearl and Kari-mi, who were playing with dolls. She felt a little old for that—but not that old, really—so she sat down with them, and the three girls had a wonderful time.

DUFFY
AND SIMEL

Duffy found herself growing more and more interested in the ways of the Masai people. She watched the warriors, of course. They were fascinating, even if she did find herself irritated that they did not do more of the work.

If they were back in America, it would be different, she thought. But then, this was not America. This was Africa, and she should not be expecting to see the same customs.

Several times Duffy and Pearl joined the Masai women when they got together to sing and dance among themselves. The women would put on colorful beaded necklaces and soft lambskin dresses for their meetings. To Duffy's surprise, some of the songs they sang were prayer songs, thanking God for His blessings. They even seemed to pray for some of the same things that Duffy herself and her family prayed for. Karimi told them that the women asked God for children, for rain, and for daily needs.

"I notice that the ladies seem to have prayer times more than the men do, Karimi," she said to her young friend one day.

"Oh yes. Women pray more than men."

"Why is that, do you suppose?"

"I don't know. Is it not true in your land?"

For a moment Duffy had to think. After a long pause, she too said, "I don't know."

"The Masai women pray a lot. Sometimes, when they begin their prayers, they will sprinkle milk in three directions—the north, the south, and the east. They have been taught that helps."

"What about the west?"

"That is where the sun sets. It is used only for curses."

"For curses!"

"Oh yes." Karimi nodded confidently. "That's only for curses."

They were sitting on the outer edge of a circle of praying women. The words of their prayers meant nothing to Duffy and Pearl, of course, until Karimi translated for them. "What are they saying today, Karimi?"

"They are saying, 'Give us children—give us cattle—our hope is with You always.'"

The meeting went on for some time.

"Do the men have prayer meetings like this?"

"Not very often. Not like this," Karimi said. "But they can't do anything that would interfere with the women's meetings."

"Well, I should think not!"

"And the men have to supply all the things that are needed—such as animals for sacrifices."

Pearl's eyes grew big. She said, "You have animal sacrifices?"

"Yes, sometimes we offer a lamb without a blemish."

Instantly Duffy saw her opportunity. "The Bible says Jesus is the true lamb without a blemish."

"Yes, I know. I've heard Naiko say so. And the missionaries say that."

"Christians don't offer real lambs to God," Pearl said. "We don't believe we need animal sacrifices. That's because Jesus is our sacrifice lamb. He died to be our sacrifice."

Karimi seemed to listen with interest while the two girls spoke to her about Jesus. But then she began talking about what the Masai people believed.

"Our people are very spiritual," she said. "When a Masai passes a holy tree, he will pluck green grass and put it on the tree and then pray. Sometimes they put necklaces or anklets there, too. And women pray for others who don't have children. That's what that woman over there is praying for now."

Duffy and Pearl looked at the woman who was

standing with her arms stretched out and tears running down her face. They could hear her praying, and Karimi told the girls what she said:

> O, God, grant to us
> The things we pray for.
> Give her the joy of motherhood.
> Let her bear and cherish.
> God give her shade to rest under,
> But not one of the tree.

"That's a beautiful prayer," Pearl whispered. "But does she know the true God?"

The two girls stayed until the praying was over, and then for a while they joined a group of boys and girls who were playing games. After that, they stopped by one of the Masai mothers' houses and found her playing with her baby.

"What's the baby's name, Karimi?" Pearl asked.

"Natoo. That's the name he is given first—the name he is given when he is a baby."

Duffy puzzled over that. "You mean he's given some different name later on?"

"Yes, that is what happens. At the first naming ceremony, both a baby and its mother have their heads shaved. A lamb is killed at that time. When the child gets to be eight years old, then he is given a second name."

"What happens to the old name?" Pearl asked.

"Oh, they keep that. So we all have two names."

"Most of us have two names in America too," Duffy said. "As well as a last name."

"Do you have naming ceremonies?" Karimi asked.

"No. Not really. Do you?"

"We do. Naming ceremonies are very important. The mother puts on her best clothes. She puts on all of her necklaces and all her earrings and heavy makeup. And all the women and the elders take part in naming the child."

"We sure don't have anything like *that* in America," Duffy said.

"And then, after they decide what name to give the baby, they bless it, and they say, 'May that name dwell in you,' and then everyone says, '*Naaii.*'"

"What does *that* mean?" Pearl asked.

"It means, 'Yes, Lord.'"

Karimi went on to talk about the rest of the naming ceremony.

And then the mother began singing to her baby.

"What's she singing, Karimi?"

"She is singing:

> Grow up, my child.
> Grow up like a mountain.
> Equal Mount Meru
> Equal Mount Kenya
> Equal Kilimanjaro
> Help your father and mother."

Duffy and Pearl and Karimi walked on. Before long, they ran into Simel.

The Masai boy looked sharply at Duffy. He made clear by his look that he did not like her very much.

Pearl asked, "Simel, why do you boys all carry sticks?"

"We begin carrying sticks when we are only three or four years old. It means we'll be herders someday. And soon after that, boys carry sticks with a sharp point on the end. That is like a warrior's spear. We use these in our play battles."

"But then don't you get hurt sometimes?" Pearl asked worriedly.

"Yes, but a Masai does not cry."

"Not even the girls?"

"Not the strong ones," Simel said. He stared at Duffy then and said, "I think you would cry."

Duffy did not answer at once. What he said was true. She had been known to cry when she was hurt. She sometimes even cried over a sad book or a sad movie. She said sharply, "There's nothing wrong with crying!"

Simel laughed. "Yes, there is—for warriors anyway!"

The youngsters walked on until they reached the open spot in the village where some games were going on. All Masai boys and girls seemed to love to play. Some of these boys had built miniature kraals. Now they were pretending that stones and sticks were sheep and cattle.

"Back home in the States, boys play with GI Joes," Pearl said.

"What is that?" Simel asked with puzzlement.

"Little statues of warriors," Duffy said, trying to find a way to explain."

This appealed to Simel. "I wish we had some of those. Do they really look like warriors?"

"Oh, yes."

"What do the girls play with?"

"They play dolls—with Barbie dolls lots of times."

"What is a Barbie doll?"

Pearl held up her hands about eight inches apart. "They're dolls that look like grown-up ladies."

"What do you do with them?"

"We change their clothes—put different kinds of dresses on them."

"That doesn't sound like much fun," Simel said. "It's more important to be a warrior."

"No, it's not, either!" Duffy said. "Women and men are just as important."

That started a big argument at once, and finally Simel just stalked off angrily.

"Why do you argue with him, Duffy?" Pearl said. "You can't change people by arguing with them."

"Well, then, how *can* we help people to change when they need to change?"

Pearl thought for a moment. "Maybe the best

way to change people is to help them and be good to them—and show them we care about them . . ."

Actually Duffy suspected that Pearl was right, but she did not want to admit it. "Well, in any case, he's wrong, and I'm right."

Little Pearl shook her head, as if she knew it was useless to argue with Duffy, who was very strong-willed. "Let's go back to camp," she said. "Let's go see what Dad is doing."

They found their father taking pictures of some herders and their cattle.

"Dad, you've taken a hundred pictures of cattle," Duffy told him. "Don't you have enough?"

"You ought to know by now, Duffy," Mr. Kerrigan said, "that I *have* to take about a hundred pictures to be sure of getting one really good one."

They followed their father around for a while, and all at once he asked, "And how are you getting along with Simel, Duffy?"

"Not very well," she admitted. "He's always wanting to argue with me."

"Maybe you're arguing with him. Did you ever think of that?"

Duffy knew that she had been wrong, and she lowered her head.

Her father put his hand on her shoulder. "You've got to learn to let people be themselves, Duffy. And that's as true back home as it is here."

"I know, Dad. It's just so hard, when I want things to be right."

Mr. Kerrigan patted his daughter's shoulder. "Well, you can do it, I'm sure. In fact, you'll have to, if you want to travel with me on these trips."

Traveling with her father meant a great deal to Duffy. As she left to wander around the *engang* by herself, she began to think about all that was happening. "I've got a problem. I've got to stop being so critical of people who are different from me," she muttered. "I know it's not right, but I just can't seem to help myself."

Duffy kicked at a rock and watched it go. Then she said, "Lord, You'll just have to change me. I want You to do it. I can't change myself."

11

BAD NEWS
FOR DUFFY

I need to talk to you, Duffy."

Duffy was walking on the outskirts of the *engang*. She looked up when her dad unexpectedly joined her. She could not help noticing at once the odd expression in his eyes.

"Let's get out of the sun under that tree," he said.

"All right, Dad."

When they were in the shade, Duffy asked, "What is it, Dad? What's up?"

"Well, I have a rather difficult thing to say to you, daughter. It's going to be hard, but I want you to take it in the right spirit."

Almost instantly Duffy knew what was coming. Her throat grew tight, but she nodded. She found she could not say a word.

"You remember when we were making our decision whether or not you and the other kids should come to Africa with me, don't you?"

"Sure, Dad, I remember."

Mr. Kerrigan hesitated. "Then, you'll remember too that I told you all that this would be sort of a trial run. If you did well, then I would think about taking you along on my other trips. But if you didn't, then you would have to stay at home, and Aunt Minnie would stay with you while I'm gone." He hesitated again, then said, "It looks like it's going to have to be that way."

"You mean we can't go on any more trips with you?"

"I'm afraid not. You, especially, just haven't been able to fit yourself into all of this, Duffy." Waving his hand around, he indicated the large plain and the round mud-covered huts of the Masai.

From now on when he traveled, they would be staying home? With Aunt Minnie? Duffy had a sick feeling in her stomach.

The bawls of the cattle sounded in the air, as a group of boys and girls dodged in and out among them, playing a game. Over to their right stood a group of elders, draped in their reddish blankets. They seemed to be having some sort of meeting. And looking beyond the men, Duffy could see the house that Tajewi was building.

"I know that life here is so different from what you're accustomed to," her dad said. "Especially

102

some of the customs. And I know it's extra hard because these people have some beliefs that go against everything we hold to be true as Christians. But I can't offend the people that I'm working with, Duffy. You can see that, can't you?"

"Yes."

"Well, I wanted to talk to you first, because the other kids have pretty well been able to keep a good relationship with the Masai. But I'm afraid you just haven't been able to do that, have you?"

"No sir."

Duffy's face twisted. She knew she was about to cry.

Her father put an arm around her and gave her a hug. "Don't cry, honey. I'll tell you what. When you're a little older, we'll try a trip again. But for now, I'm afraid it'll have to be another way."

Again, Duffy could not say a word. Her throat was tight, and she had to blink to hold back the tears.

Her father gave her another hug and walked off toward their campsite.

Blindly Duffy turned and went off in the other direction. *Why did I have to act the way I did?* she thought. *Why couldn't I have just kept my big mouth shut when I saw something I didn't like?*

Duffy kept to herself the rest of the day. She was absolutely miserable. She was sitting on a small hill that overlooked the *engang,* just thinking about all the trouble she had caused, when she saw Juan coming. He looked very ticked off about something. She guessed what it was.

"Dad just told us that we're going to have to go home and stay with Aunt Minnie!" he said at once.

"Yes. I know. He told me."

"And it's all your fault, Duffy!" Juan said crossly. Ordinarily Juan was a very cheerful boy, and Duffy could tell that he was terribly disappointed. "If you just hadn't shot your mouth off about the Masai eating blood and tried to straighten them out on how many wives a man can have and everything else you didn't like—if you hadn't done that, all this wouldn't have happened!"

"I know it, Juan. I know. I'm sorry."

Juan shook his head in disgust. "That's a big help now!" he snorted. "Now all we've got to look forward to is Aunt Minnie!"

He stomped off, and Duffy felt even worse—if that were possible. She got up and began wandering back through the village. Before long she was going by the home of Karimi and Simel.

"Hello, Duffy." Karimi was wearing her usual garment, a kind of red toga. "How are you this day?"

Duffy wanted to say, "I'm terrible," but she forced herself to smile. "Oh, I'm doing all right. And how are you?"

"I'm very well. Would you like to do something with me for a while today?" Karimi smiled.

"Yes, I would," Duffy said quickly. It did not

matter what Karimi wanted to do. Duffy was determined she was going to change her ways.

"Good. Then come into our house. I have to get some things."

Duffy followed Karimi into the loaf-shaped house. It had only one room. There was one bed—large enough for six people to sleep on—and there was one much smaller. That was a bed for the mother of the house and her very young children. The beds were made with branches from trees and were covered with soft cowhide. In the very center of the house was a hearth, which was used for cooking, for warmth, and for light.

But along the side of the room was the strangest thing of all. It was a fenced-off place for newborn calves or goats. The fence barrier separated the animal place from the rest of the house. There were no true windows, but an opening in the walls and another one in the roof let the light in and the smoke out.

"I have to go gather some fruit, Duffy. You can help me with that. Do you want to?"

"Oh yes. I can do that," Duffy said eagerly. She followed Karimi outside, and the girl led her to the very edge of the village. Over in the distance were the huge forms of the mountains surrounding the valley. "What big mountain is that?" Duffy asked. It rose high into the air. It was snow-covered.

"Oh, that is Oldoinyo le Engai."

"Does that mean something special?"

"It means the Mountain of God. My father says it's a lone candle, a gift from God, and we must worship in its shadow and pray for cattle and children."

Duffy asked, "Have you heard much about Jesus, Karimi?"

"Oh yes. My Uncle Naiko, he tells us all about Jesus. I love to hear of the stories of Jesus. Did you know He healed the sick people?"

"Yes," Duffy said, "I do know that." And again she began to talk about the Lord to the little Masai girl. She talked as they made their way toward a large tree. She spoke of how she herself had trusted Jesus just a year earlier and how she was trying to please Him.

"I will be a Christian someday, I think," Karimi said firmly. "It will be hard, because my people love the old ways. But you can tell me more about Jesus anytime you want to. I like to hear."

And Duffy kept on doing that as they picked the fruit, strange fruit that looked a little like sausages. Finally Karimi said they had gathered enough, and they carried their full baskets back to the hut.

"Now we must squeeze them out into the calabash," she said.

Duffy helped Karimi press the fruit into what looked just like a large gourd. After a while she asked, "What will this be, Karimi? What are we getting ready to make?"

"Oh, this will make honey beer."

Duffy had to bite her lip. She knew that every Masai drank the mild form of beer they called honey beer. She almost said, "I think it's wrong to drink beer." But she didn't say that. She had learned a little, and now she simply swallowed and said, "Let me help you do some other things too."

The rest of the afternoon she worked with Karimi. They went out and pulled up long strands of lion grass, and Karimi taught her to weave them together with leather thongs. This made the mats that the Masai used in their houses to pen up the baby animals.

The girls were still busy working on the mats when Naiko suddenly appeared. "Hello, young women," he said. He smiled broadly and looked very handsome. "What have you been doing today?"

"Duffy has been helping me pick fruit and make honey beer and weave mats," Karimi said. "She is very good at helping, too."

Naiko gave Duffy a pleased look and sat down beside them. He watched them work for a while. When Karimi left to get more grass, he said, "I am glad to see that you are getting along well with my niece Karimi."

"She's such a sweet girl, Naiko. I like her very much. I've been talking to her about Jesus a lot today."

Looking pleased, Naiko said, "That is good, Duffy. That is good. I myself have told her how Jesus changed my life. I think one day she and her brother both will become Christians. Then their father will see what Jesus can do." He sighed and said, "It is a slow way. I would like to see every Masai follow Jesus at once, but it is very difficult." He looked then toward the beautiful mountains and murmured, "The Mountain of God."

"I know," Duffy said with a smile. "Karimi told me."

Sadness seemed to come over Naiko then. "Our Masai way of life is passing. One day *engangs* such as this will be no more."

"But why, Naiko?"

"It is a matter of land. Years ago the Masai owned all this land, you see. But now the white man has encouraged settlers to come and live here. Every year we have less land. But it takes much land for our cattle, Duffy, and we are losing it bit by bit."

This made Duffy very sad too, until she thought of something else. Suddenly she looked up at the tall warrior and said, "I know that makes you sad, but the Bible says that we have a place in heaven waiting for us—a house that isn't made with hands."

"Does the Bible indeed say those words?" Naiko stared at her. "I did not know that."

"Yes, it does. We're just sort of travelers here,

it says. It's like we're passing through. And one day we'll be at our real home with Jesus."

"You are a good preacher, my little one," he said. "You keep on speaking to my niece."

"I will do that," Duffy promised. But then she bit her lip. "But I have offended Simel, Naiko. He will not be so easy to talk to."

But Naiko said, "You will know what you must do. I have great confidence in you."

The big Masai left then, and soon Karimi came back with a new supply of grass. The two girls busied themselves with their mat making.

After the Kerrigans' evening meal and their daily family Bible time, Duffy said she was going to bed early. But she lay awake for a long time. She began to pray again that the Lord would give her a different attitude.

"Oh, God, I've been so wrong," she prayed. "And I'm sorry. I want to be able to accept people. I don't have to accept their ways in order to accept *them*. And, Lord, I do love the Masai people, but I'm afraid that Simel hates me. I've been so terrible to him."

She lay listening to the sounds of the African night and asking God to show her what to do about Simel. Finally she thought she knew. She said, "Amen," and went to sleep.

THE
PERFECT ENDING

When Duffy got up the next morning, her mind was made up. She must have been extra quiet or else didn't eat as much breakfast as usual, for Juan said, "What's the matter with you?"

"Nothing," Duffy said quickly.

"I hope you're not coming down with something," Mr. Kerrigan said with a worried look on his face. "These African fevers can be pretty serious."

"No, I feel fine, Daddy. Really."

Duffy looked across from where their tents were set up and saw that a group of the older boys were already playing. Simel was one of them, and she knew that the time had come. As soon as breakfast was over, she said, "I want all of you kids to come with me. Will you?"

"Come where?" Seth asked, frowning.

"Please. I wish you would all come. You too, Dad. I've got to do something, and I want you all to hear it."

Pearl must have sensed what was going on. Right away she agreed. "Sure. I'll go with you."

"We'll all go," Seth said.

Duffy got up and walked across the rolling ground. Pearl walked beside her and took her hand. Duffy smiled down at her and said, "You're a good sister, Pearl."

"So are you," Pearl answered with her big smile.

They reached the edge of the playing field, and all of the boys stopped their game and looked at the Kerrigan family. Duffy saw that there was not a friendly look on Simel's face, but she did not let that stop her. She walked right up to him and said, "Simel, I want to say something to you."

"What is it you don't like about us this time?" he asked harshly.

Duffy swallowed hard. "I didn't come to say anything like that. I wanted to tell you . . ."

She hesitated. She saw that all of the boys were listening. She saw that the girls who had been watching the boys' game were very obser-vant, too. Everybody knew about the thoughtless things she had said. Then she glanced back and saw her father watching her closely and a little anxiously. Seth and Juan also seemed to be some-what worried.

She turned back to Simel. "Well, I've been very wrong," Duffy said, looking the boy straight in the eye. "And I wanted to tell you that. I have made unkind remarks about you and about your way of life. I wish I could take them back. But after words are said, there's no way to take them back again." She lowered her head.

And then Duffy noticed a small plant growing at her feet. It was white and fluffy like an old dandelion. She pulled it up, blew on it, and the wind took the seeds all away. "It is as hard to gather up all the unkind words that I said as it would be to gather all those seeds. But I want to tell you that I am *very* sorry for the way I've acted. I was wrong, and I have asked God to forgive me. And I now ask you to forgive me."

Total silence fell over the group. No one said a single word. But when Duffy looked at her father, she saw that there was pride in his eyes. He nodded and gave her a victory gesture with his hand.

Simel kept studying Duffy's face. He seemed to be thinking hard. After a moment he said, "Do you really mean what you said?"

"I meant what I said, and I'll do anything to prove it."

"All right, then. Come and eat something at my house."

Somehow Duffy knew right away what was coming. She had made too many remarks about the Masai habit of eating blood and how awful it was. Glancing around the circle of watching boys and girls, she saw the Masai youngsters nudge each other. They knew, of course. *Simel would have told them,* she thought.

"All right, Simel. I'll come and eat something at your house."

"Come, then," Simel said.

They made quite a parade—first Duffy and Simel; then all the other boys and girls. The rest of the Kerrigans trailed behind. By the side of one of the many kraals, they found Naiko talking with his brother, the Masai who was Simel and Karimi's father.

"This girl wants to eat some of our food, Father," Simel said.

Simel's father looked much surprised. "That is fine. But why would she want to do that?"

"I think I know, brother," Naiko said. "It is all right. Let them do as they say."

"Very well. What food would you like?"

"Just some milk with—" Simel hesitated, then grinned slyly "—with just a little blood in it, if you please."

Simel's father must have just finished milking the cow, because a jug of fresh milk sat by the kraal. Now he took a small blade and drew a little blood from the cow to add to the milk.

Naiko took the jug and shook it to mix the

114

contents. He poured a little milk into a drinking gourd.

Now every eye was fixed on Duffy, and she was afraid that she could not go through with this. Silently she prayed, *Lord, I really don't want to do this, but I want to prove to these people that I'm really sorry for the way I've acted. So help me to keep this down.*

Juan was standing close by. He nudged her and said, "Makes me think about what Jesus told the disciples—if they drank any deadly thing, it wouldn't hurt them."

"Thank you, Juan."

Closing her eyes, Duffy took the small gourd and lifted it to her lips. Without hesitating, she took four or five long swallows, closing her mind to the taste. Actually, she decided, she could not really tell any difference. It tasted just like milk to her. She handed the gourd to Simel and said, "Thank you, Simel. That was very good milk."

To Duffy's surprise, a round of cheers went up. All of the Masai youngsters were applauding her. They must have known how hard it was for one not raised as a Masai to drink something so very different.

And then Duffy's family surrounded her. They all hugged her so hard that she finally had to say, "You're smothering me!"

"I'm very proud of you, daughter," her father told her.

"So am I," Juan said.

Seth gave her an extra hard hug. "You're a fine sister."

And then Pearl came up and threw her arms around Duffy. "I'm so proud of you, Duffy."

"Never should have happened in the first place," Duffy muttered.

Naiko heard her and said, "Daughter, do not grieve over wrongs done in the past, when they have been forgiven. You cannot change them any more than you can gather the seeds of the thistle. Just go on and resolve never to let anything like that ever happen again."

The rest of the morning turned out to be great fun. The Masai boys allowed the Kerrigan kids to play in their ball game. Again, it was a rough game. Each of them was knocked down at one time or another. One time Duffy went down so hard that she got a small cut in her forehead.

She knew that Simel was watching to see if she would get angry, as she had before. But she jumped up, dabbed at the bleeding scrape, and said, "It's just a little cut. Let's play some more."

When the game ended, Simel walked over to Duffy. "You would make a good Masai," he said.

Duffy Kerrigan grinned. "That's the nicest thing anyone has ever said to me, Simel."

The Kerrigans were all packed, their gear was in the trailer, and the engine of the Land Rover was running. Mr. Kerrigan had finished taking his pictures, and it was time to go home.

"When you are grown up, I want you to come back," Simel told Duffy. "I want you to see a real Masai warrior. Me."

Duffy felt a lump in her throat as she looked around at the big Masai warriors. She looked at the women, who stood smiling at her. Then she looked at all the boys and girls who had gathered. She had grown to be great friends with Simel and Karimi and many others too. Now she must leave them. The parting was hard.

As the Land Rover pulled away, all the Kerrigans waved. The warriors, the women, and the boys and girls all were singing a good-bye song for them. And then Duffy heard Simel's voice hollering, "Come back when you grow up, Duffy, and see a real Masai warrior! *Me!*"

As they bumped along over the dusty road, the huge blue mountain hovered over them. Duffy looked at it and said, "I'll never forget this place as long as I live."

"Neither will I," Juan said. "Let's come back sometime."

"Maybe we will," Mr. Kerrigan said. "Maybe we will." Then he looked over at Juan and asked, "Why are you scratching yourself?"

"Because I'm the only one that knows where I itch," Juan said.

His father groaned. "Always a wisecrack. I

hope you get some better jokes before we go on our next trip."

Suddenly every Kerrigan youngster was alert.

"The next trip!" Duffy cried. "Are we getting to go with you on your next trip, Dad?"

"Yes, I'm pleased to say that you are. And very soon, too. I've seen some changes in this family that tell me you're ready." Then he looked into the rearview mirror and smiled right at Duffy.

"Where are we going?" Seth asked eagerly. "Not back to Africa?"

"Nope. This time we're going to—" He stopped, then said, "But maybe I shouldn't tell you yet."

A series of cries filled the Land Rover, and Mr. Kerrigan held up one hand. "All right. I'll tell you. Don't make such a fuss about it." He put both hands on the wheel as they dodged a bump, then said, "We're going to England."

"To England! Hooray!" Juan said. "I've always wanted to go to England."

"Well, I've got an assignment to do a story and take pictures in England. So we'll go home and rest awhile, and then we'll take off for London."

Duffy leaned back in her seat and was quiet for a time. Finally she said, "Well, I made such a mess of this trip. I hope I don't offend the English people as bad as I did the Masai."

"Aw, you won't," Juan said. "You'll probably win a gold medal for your good behavior." His face lit up, and he said, "Say, did you hear about the dumb athlete that won a gold medal at the Olympics?"

Duffy rolled her eyes. "No, but I know you're going to tell us about him. And I already know it'll be an awful joke."

"He took it home and had it bronzed. Isn't that a doozy?"

The Kerrigans bounced happily up and down as the Land Rover rumbled over the bumps.

After a while Pearl leaned close to Duffy and murmured, "I'm glad you made things right with the Masai kids, Duffy. And Karimi told me how you talked to her about Jesus. Well, I talked to her, too. And we prayed together, and she asked Jesus to come into her heart."

"Did she really? How wonderful!" Duffy exclaimed. "That makes our trip just perfect."

The flight home to the States was tiring, but when they stepped inside their front door, the first thing Juan said was, "All right, unpack and then get packed again. We're off for England."

"Give us a break, Juan," Duffy said. "We need to wash clothes first."

"All the rest of you need to practice up on how you talk. I already speak with a perfect English accent." Seth grinned.

Duffy laughed with the rest, but she was thinking, *It's going to be wonderful to go to London.*

I'll get to watch them change the guard at Buckingham Palace, and I'll . . .

A warm, good feeling went over Duffy, and her busy mind began thinking of what interesting people she would meet in England.

Get swept away in the many Gilbert Morris Adventures available from Moody Press:

"Too Smart" Jones

4025-8 Pool Party Thief
4026-6 Buried Jewels
4027-4 Disappearing Dogs
4028-2 Dangerous Woman
4029-0 Stranger in the Cave
4030-4 Cat's Secret
4031-2 Stolen Bicycle
4032-0 Wilderness Mystery
4033-9 Spooky Mansion
4034-7 Mysterious Artist

Come along for the adventures and mysteries Juliet "Too Smart" Jones always manages to find. She and her other homeschool friends solve these great adventures and learn biblical truths along the way. Ages 9-14

Seven Sleepers - The Lost Chronicles

3667-6 The Spell of the Crystal Chair
3668-4 The Savage Game of Lord Zarak
3669-2 The Strange Creatures of Dr. Korbo
3670-6 City of the Cyborgs
3671-4 The Temptations of Pleasure Island
3672-2 Victims of Nimbo
3673-0 The Terrible Beast of Zor

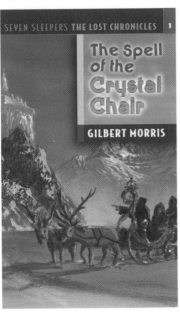

More exciting adventures from the Seven Sleepers. As these exciting young people attempt to faithfully follow Goél, they learn important moral and spiritual lessons. Come along with them as they encounter danger, intrigue, and mystery. Ages 10-14

Dixie Morris Animal Adventures

Follow the exciting adventures of this animal lover as she learns more of God and His character through her many adventures underneath the Big Top.
Ages 9-14

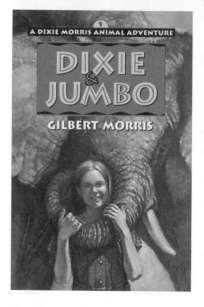

The Daystar Voyages

Join the crew of the Daystar as they traverse the wide expanse of space. Adventure and danger abound, but they learn time and again that God is truly the Master of the Universe.
Ages 10-14

MOODY
The Name You Can Trust
1-800-678-8812 www.MoodyPress.org

Seven Sleepers Series

3681-1 Flight of the Eagles
3682-X The Gates of Neptune
3683-3 The Swords of Camelot
3684-6 The Caves That Time
        Forgot
3685-4 Winged Riders of the
        Desert
3686-2 Empress of the
        Underworld
3687-0 Voyage of the Dolphin
3691-9 Attack of the Amazons
3692-7 Escape with the Dream
        Maker
3693-5 The Final Kingdom

Go with Josh and his friends as they are sent by Goél, their spiritual leader, on dangerous and challenging voyages to conquer the forces of darkness in the new world. Ages 10-14

Bonnets and Bugles Series

0911-3 Drummer Boy at Bull
        Run
0912-1 Yankee Belles in Dixie
0913-X The Secret of Richmond
        Manor
0914-8 The Soldier Boy's
        Discovery
0915-6 Blockade Runner
0916-4 The Gallant Boys of
        Gettysburg
0917-2 The Battle of Lookout
        Mountain
0918-0 Encounter at Cold
        Harbor
0919-9 Fire Over Atlanta
0920-2 Bring the Boys Home

Follow good friends Leah Carter and Jeff Majors as they experience danger, intrigue, compassion, and love in these civil war adventures. Ages 10-14

MOODY
The Name You Can Trust
1-800-678-8812 www.MoodyPress.org